THE ECHO AND THE VOICE

THE ECHO AND THE VOICE

J.W. Kindbloom

Cover and interior design by Chloe Manolis

Editing by Mark E. Firehammer, Katrina D. Hawley

ISBN: 979-8-9994752-1-3

Published by Firehammer Publishing, Holyoke, Massachusetts

For those who heard something true in themselves—and followed it, even when the world called it foolish.

"Don't ask yourself what the world needs. Ask yourself what makes you come alive, and go do that. Because what the world needs is people who have come alive."

—Howard Thurman

Prologue - The First Memory

Some memories come before language.
Some truths are born before we know how to name them.

Long before Jonas had words, he had this.

A memory—not sharp, but vivid. Not something he could explain, but something that lived in him, like breath.

He was small—smaller than thought, smaller than fear. The world around him was shadow and warmth and the soft rush of unseen movement. And then, a light—not blinding, but endless. Like the color of morning before the sun finds its edge.

From within the light came a presence. Familiar. Loved.

Not in the way a child knows a mother's arms, but deeper. Older.

A man stood there, smiling—a sadness in his eyes so deep it almost shimmered. Jonas didn't know him. And yet he did. The man knelt, bringing his face close. His lips moved. The words, as they floated toward Jonas, didn't pass through his ears. They arrived directly inside him, like the way warmth moves through skin, or how a dream moves through sleep.

"This voice you hear—never let it go."

Behind the man's voice, there was another—a quieter thread, steady and clear, weaving through everything. Jonas could feel it even then: a kind of music beneath the music, a current beneath the water.

The man's smile faltered for a moment, and sorrow passed across him like a shadow. Jonas didn't understand the sorrow, but he recognized its weight. The man touched Jonas's hand, light as a falling leaf.

"You will hear the Echo," the man said.
"It will speak louder and louder. It will promise you safety, praise, belonging. But it will ask for a price. It will ask for your Voice."

Jonas felt the man's sadness tighten, as if the very memory of that price was too much to carry.

"I made that mistake," the man whispered. "I traded truth for comfort. And it cost me everything. Please—when you hear the Echo calling, remember: the Voice is quiet. But it is real. Follow it."

Jonas did not know what promises meant. He did not know what loss was. But somewhere deep inside, something folded itself into place—a seed, waiting.

The man pressed his forehead to Jonas's for a moment. And then he was gone, like mist dissolving into light.

The memory would not fade.

It would live inside Jonas, growing with him, whispering alongside every heartbeat:

>*The Voice never shouts. But it always speaks.*

And even before he had words, Jonas was already listening.

Interlude - The Echo and the Voice

The Echo was already here.

Not born with us—but waiting for us, in systems long established.

It echoes still: in the rules passed down without question, in the praise of obedience, in the illusion of normal.

It tells us who to be before we know who we are.

It sounds like belonging.

Until we remember what came first.

The Voice came first.

You're born with it.

Before the names, before the noise.

It asks nothing but presence.

It doesn't shout. But it always speaks.

Part I: Echo and the Rebel

The voice begins not as a sound, but as a refusal.

Chapter 1 – The First Song

The smell of coffee, patchouli, and sage drifted through the air, wrapping around Jonas like an invisible embrace. The wooden floors of the small coffeehouse creaked beneath his feet as he followed his older sister, Elaine—nearly fifteen, seven years his senior—through clusters of people who looked so different from the world he knew at home.

It was summer and they had just moved to this Gulf Coast town from Massachusetts. The air was heavier here, thick with warmth even at night, but the coffeehouse felt like another world entirely—one that felt safe in a way Jonas wasn't that familiar with. It was a place where voices hummed with excitement, where laughter came easily, and being different didn't seem to bother anyone. Whatever this was, it felt good, Jonas thought—and it stirred something deeper than he had words for. It was something he wanted to explore, curious to see where it might lead.

The summer before Jonas had learned how unpredictable people could be. The neighbor boys sometimes played baseball with him in the yard or came over to play ping-pong on the table he'd built himself from leftover wood in his father's basement. But other times—without warning—they would drag him behind the barn and drop him into the dark, flooded crawlspace beneath it.

*
**

It was a dangerous place, especially to a six-year-old. Water pooled over broken boards, rusted metal, and old furniture left to rot. Jagged pieces of forgotten things jutted out at odd angles beneath the surface. Light slashed through the gaps in the barn's wooden skirt in narrow streaks, making the shadows seem to shift and flicker like something alive. His mind, rich with imagination, filled in the rest: snakes, nails, monsters—things that might be waiting just out of sight.

Of course, at six, Jonas couldn't understand why the boys did it. It was his first experience with cruelty disguised as play. He never knew which version of them he'd meet—the ones who laughed with him or the ones who held his arms too tight. That confusion left a mark. It taught him that people's comfort with difference came and went like the weather—and sometimes, being different made you a target.

*
**

Jonas moved through the coffeehouse, soaking in every detail like a sponge. The candles flickered in empty wine bottles, their soft light bouncing off the chipped tabletops. Steam curled from ceramic mugs, tracing wisps into the air. An acoustic guitar thrummed in the corner, each string vibrating like a heartbeat. Jonas didn't just feel at home—he felt connected to something bigger.

Elaine, barely noticed him. She had bigger things on her mind—older boys, the thrill of independence, the excitement of being part of something. Jonas liked it that way. She had to bring him along when their parents told her to babysit, but she didn't try to control him. He could do whatever he wanted, as long as he didn't distract or embarrass her.

*
**

A girl—probably no older than fourteen or fifteen—stepped onto the small stage, holding a folded piece of paper in her hands. She cleared her throat, glancing nervously at the audience before beginning to read.

The tulips are too excitable, it is winter here.
Look how white everything is, how quiet, how snowed-in.
I am learning peacefulness, lying by myself quietly
As the light lies on these white walls, this bed, these hands.

The words slid through the room like a slow-moving current, and Jonas felt something inside him tighten. Snowed-in. The phrase tugged at his memory, pulling him back to Massachusetts, where the world would turn white in winter, where the last stubborn pile of snow behind the garage would shrink day by day until only a spoonful remained.

*
**

Tulips.

He remembered them pushing up through the thawing earth, their colors bold and deep, as if the world had been holding its breath all winter just to release them. He had always been mesmerized by them—the way their petals folded around something unseen, a secret held in red and orange and gold. He would sit on the cold ground and stare at them, trying to understand their mystery. He didn't yet know how much life would try to press him back down.

The girl continued reading, her voice soft but sure, but Jonas had already drifted somewhere else. The poem was sad —he could tell, even if he didn't fully understand it. But to him, tulips weren't sad at all. They were alive. They were defiant.

Jonas dug into his pocket and pulled out the stub of a pencil he carried. He grabbed a napkin from the table and, pressing against the uneven wooden surface, began to write down his own thoughts about tulips—not dark, not heavy, but bright and bursting with life. They didn't hide from the cold or shrink under pressure. They pushed up from the hard, frozen earth, refusing to stay buried, opening themselves wide to the sky as if daring the world to look away. Jonas felt a flicker of recognition, as if the flower was telling him something about himself—about how it felt to push through and stand out in a world that seemed determined to stay gray and quiet.

No one noticed.

They don't ask the snow if it's okay
Don't wait for the sun to say "go play"
They just come up—red and bold
Through chilly dirt that still feels cold

He looked down at what he'd written, then folded the napkin carefully and tucked it into his pocket. It wasn't much —but it was his. And something told him it might matter later.

*
**

Elaine was busy flirting with a boy leaning against the counter. The audience was caught up in the poetry, in the music, in the electricity of the moment.
Jonas liked it that way. He could just be.

The afternoon stretched on, one performer after another taking the stage. Poets. Singers. A man telling a story so wild Jonas wasn't sure whether it was real or just made up on the spot. He didn't care. It was his kind of magic.

*
**

But all magic had an ending. At some point, Elaine nudged him. "Time to head back for dinner."

Jonas wanted to stay. The air was alive with stories and songs, and he wanted to hold onto that feeling. But he knew he'd be back, and in the meantime, he would archive every detail in his mind, like collecting souvenirs of inspiration. He never knew when he'd need them later.

*
**

The scent of sage and coffee lingered in his clothes as they stepped outside, the golden light of early evening spilling over the quiet streets. The sounds of the coffeehouse faded behind them as they walked toward home, the heat of the day still holding on, making the air feel thick and slow.

Jonas knew they wouldn't talk about the coffeehouse at dinner. His family didn't talk about much. His father's presence at the table was like a heavy stone, unyielding and unmoved. Conversation wasn't forbidden—it just didn't happen, as if the air itself decided to stay quiet. Jonas had learned that people only spoke when they had something useful to say—or at least that's how his father saw it.

Questions weren't asked. Opinions weren't offered. He knew his father wasn't interested in what Jonas thought or felt

—only in whether he was following the rules. Elaine would usually respond with one-word answers, just enough to avoid notice. Rachel mostly stayed quiet, watching everything, sensing which way the wind was blowing before deciding what to say—if anything. Jonas knew how to gauge his father's mood without saying anything, reading his body language like a familiar script.

But inside, his thoughts burned bright, like tulips pushing up through the last melting snow.

Chapter 2 – The Factory Visit

Jonas stood on the concrete floor of the factory, his eyes wide and curious, taking in the machinery, the constant hum, and the workers moving like cogs in a giant, unfeeling machine. The smell of oil and metal hung in the air, sharp and unforgiving. Light seemed to come from everywhere, bathing the vast space in a strange, shadow-less glow. Jonas marveled at how the room seemed to have no darkness at all—just an even, relentless brightness that made everything feel exposed and inescapable.

His father barely said a word on the drive over. When Jonas had asked why he was tagging along, his father just mumbled something about it being good for him to see "real work.

Jonas had a feeling he knew what this was really about. The coffeehouse napkin. The one he'd scrawled those lines about tulips refusing to wait. He had copied the lines into a small notebook he kept hidden in the back of his desk drawer, a place for thoughts he wasn't ready to share. But then what? Had he absentmindedly slipped the napkin back into his jeans pocket, where it might have fallen out in the laundry room? Or maybe his mother had set it on the counter. However it happened, his father had seen it. And even if he never said a word, Jonas recognized the pattern. This wasn't about filling time. It was a correction.

Jonas made a note to be more careful next time. The Echo was always watching, and the Voice was easiest to protect when it stayed hidden, at least for now.

*
**

When they arrived, his father dropped him off with a burly man named Lester. Lester looked down at Jonas, his rough hands wiping grease onto his already stained coveralls, and gave a nod. "Boss says I'm supposed to show you around," Lester said, his voice a low rumble.

Jonas just nodded, noting the way his father gave a brief, almost imperceptible look to Lester before wandering off into the gray monotony of the factory floor. Jonas couldn't help but feel that this had been arranged in advance—like his father had worked something out with Lester without saying it outright. He didn't know what the plan was, but he understood enough to know that he wasn't supposed to ask.

Lester led him through the vast space, pointing out the different stations where workers cut, shaped, and assembled the pieces that would become windows and doors. Jonas was captivated by the movement of the production line—the rhythmic clanking and whirring, the conveyor belts feeding parts into skilled hands, the careful alignment of panes and frames. It was like a machine with a heartbeat, steady and relentless.

He wanted to ask questions about how it all worked—why each step mattered, how the pieces came together to make something new—but he'd already noticed how little Lester seemed inclined to talk. Instead of trying and failing to draw him out, Jonas kept his curiosity to himself and watched everything intently, absorbing the process without demanding explanations.

One station caught his attention—a worker applying a bead of sealant to each window frame before passing it down the line. The man looked exhausted, his eyes dark and sunken, his movements almost automatic. Jonas didn't know how to explain it, but there was a sadness about him— something worn and defeated.

But not everyone looked that way. As they moved to another station, he saw a younger man carefully inspecting a finished door, giving a slight nod of satisfaction before wiping it down and adding it to the completed stack. There was a calmness about him—a sense of purpose that seemed to fit.

Jonas wasn't sure, but it seemed like the difference might have something to do with how well someone fit the rhythm of the work.

Some people moved like they belonged here, their hands steady and practiced, their faces set with quiet determination. Others looked lost, like their minds were somewhere else, fighting against every passing minute.

Jonas shifted his gaze to another worker—a woman stacking finished pieces onto a cart. She moved quickly but without energy, her face blank and distant, as if her thoughts were miles away. A couple of workers nearby muttered to each other during a lull, talking about bills piling up and how there was never enough time to get anything done at home. One of them complained about his aching back, and the other just shook his head, too tired to even commiserate.

Jonas couldn't help but wonder about the difference. He understood the coffeehouse wasn't work—not the kind that paid bills or built things—but still, the way people carried themselves there felt different—awake and alive, like the stories they told mattered. He couldn't imagine most of these factory workers sitting in that coffeehouse—or even noticing the hum of conversation, the glow of candlelight, or the way words seemed to dance through the air.

As that thought settled, Jonas looked again at the workers

—really looked. He scanned their faces, noting the weary way they moved, how their eyes seemed to track nothing in particular. It struck him that maybe it wasn't the work itself that was wrong—it was the way it swallowed people whole when it didn't fit who they were. When the work gave nothing back, it appeared to drain a person's spirit, leaving them worn and hollow, just going through the motions.

Jonas didn't feel fear or dread—just a kind of cold clarity, like stepping into water that was deeper than he'd expected.

When they finally reached the end of the tour, Lester just gave a nod and wandered back to his post, and Jonas found his father waiting for him by the door. His father looked down at him, his face impassive, and said, "See that? That's what real work looks like."

Jonas didn't respond. He wasn't sure what he was supposed to feel—pride? Gratitude? Acceptance? But none of it fit. Instead, he felt a quiet resolve take root inside him—a certainty that this wasn't his path. He didn't need to argue or resist; he just knew that his life wouldn't end up here. It was as if his father's words washed over him without sticking, like rain on stone.

As they drove home, his father stayed quiet, and Jonas knew better than to fill the silence. He had learned long ago that pushing back against his father's ideas wasn't worth the effort. His father didn't talk much, and when he did, it wasn't to ask or to wonder—it was to declare, like he was setting rules for how the world was supposed to work. Jonas figured that was fine for his father, but it wasn't how he saw things. He didn't need to agree or disagree; he just needed to observe and understand.

Deep down, Jonas knew it already—there was another way. He just had to find it.

As the silence of the drive stretched on, his hand rested absently in his lap, fingers brushing the denim of his jeans. His thoughts drifted to the small notebook hidden in the back of his desk drawer—the one no one knew about. A place for words that didn't fit here.

Chapter 3 – First Notes of Defiance

By now, Jonas had begun to recognize the shape of traps. Some came wrapped in friendship, others dressed as rules. He'd learned that a trap wasn't always a place— sometimes it was a feeling: the tightening around your choices, the quiet pressure to be someone you weren't. His father's world was one of those traps—rules followed or broken, useful or wasted, right or wrong. But Jonas had already started looking for other ways through.

Jonas's first quiet defiance came in third grade. One evening, his father announced that the school band program was starting and that Jonas would be joining. Without warning, he gave Jonas two minutes to decide which instrument he would play. Jonas didn't freeze. He didn't panic. He simply watched his father, curious—almost analytical. This wasn't about music anymore; it was a test. Not of him, but of time and control. He knew he wanted to play the trumpet, had known for a while. But the way the question was delivered—with a countdown, like a trap— sparked something else in him. A question.

What would happen if he waited? Not long. Just a few seconds. Would his father really follow through? Would the consequence match the countdown?

So he waited—two minutes and five seconds. Then said, "Trumpet."

His father's response was immediate and icy. "Too late. You didn't follow instructions. You missed your opportunity."

Jonas said nothing. Not out of fear—by now, he was used to the rules and their punishments—but because he already understood the pattern. His father believed he was teaching a lesson, but Jonas was learning something else: the boundaries, the limits, the blind spots. His father thought he'd closed a door, but Jonas was already looking for another way in.

*
**

A few days later, Jonas found himself flipping through his mother's S&H Green Stamps catalog—the kind she kept tucked away in the kitchen cupboard. He had no plan when he started, just a sense of curiosity and the hum of unfinished business in his chest. And then he saw it: a brass bugle.

The solution appeared as if it had been waiting for him. He didn't need his father's approval to play an instrument—he just needed the right tool and a path of his own. The bugle had no valves, no complex fingerings. It required only breath, lips, and control. And that's where Jonas set his focus.

The bugle wasn't a secret—he practiced when his father was at work, and his mother never stopped him—but it felt like his. A strategy, not a workaround. He threw himself into learning how to produce clean notes, experimenting with lip tension and breath support. He stood in the backyard when the neighbors were gone, sending clear, bold tones into the open air. Sometimes he imagined they echoed farther than he could hear.

When the fourth grade came around, his father posed the question again—this time without warning. "They're choosing instruments next week. You've got two minutes, Jonas. What'll it be?" Jonas didn't flinch. "Trumpet," he said, well within the time limit. His father nodded, satisfied—never guessing how prepared Jonas already was. He said it without pause, already knowing the rules. He'd learned what happened when you waited. But even then, some part of him wondered if, eventually, the rules might take away the chance to choose for himself.

Everyone could be in band—there were no tryouts, just sign-ups. On the first day of class, the band director went around the room helping each student learn their first notes. But when he got to Jonas and heard the clarity and tone of his sound, he paused. Jonas's breath control and embouchure were already so developed that it immediately set him apart.

Within a week, the director moved Jonas to the intermediate group—something that rarely happened so early. From that point on, throughout elementary and into high school, Jonas was rarely anywhere but first or second chair.

Music became a place where his efforts were recognized not because he followed the rules, but because he understood them—then quietly found a better way. That year affirmed something vital in him: he didn't need permission to grow. If the door was closed, he'd find a window—or build one himself.

That confidence carried into other parts of his life, too. He began to trust his own timing, his instincts, his need to understand before agreeing. It wasn't rebellion for rebellion's sake. It was something subtler, deeper—a personal blueprint taking shape.

Even as his world grew more complex, Jonas never forgot that year. The bugle became more than an instrument; it was a symbol of his ability to adapt, to learn under his own terms, and to come out stronger because of it.

Chapter 4 – First Lessons in Belonging

For Jonas, the next couple of years unfolded not as experiments, but as a series of first lessons. — quiet moments that shaped Jonas's understanding of what it meant to belong. Sixth grade marked the final year of elementary school, and with it came an unspoken expectation: that he would find his footing among his peers, align with the rules of childhood social life, and wade more deeply into the unavoidable currents of the Echo. Jonas, equipped with his own unique compass, trusted himself to navigate those currents without losing the quiet thread that guided him.

*
**

In Jonas's family, the idea of pets had always been an unspoken impossibility. Pets were not part of life, they were told — a sentiment his father reinforced with dry jokes about how dogs were good for little more than a kick. Over time, the children had resigned themselves to this reality, accepting that tenderness toward animals was something for other families, not theirs.

So when the announcement came that they would be

visiting the local animal shelter, it landed like a minor miracle —an invitation into a world they had been taught was not theirs to enter. Clearly, conversations had taken place behind closed doors, but as usual, the children were simply along for the ride.

At the animal shelter, Jonas watched with quiet amazement as a small, scrappy cat named Cecil made an immediate connection with his father—a moment of connection so swift and genuine that it left an imprint on Jonas's young heart. Still, they left empty-handed, driving slowly down the long gravel driveway.

Jonas sat silently in the back seat, feeling the pull of something unresolved. Then, almost imperceptibly, the car began to slow. His father's hands gripped the wheel, his jaw tightened, and finally, he said the words that seemed almost too delicate to come from him: "We have to go back and get Cecil."

No one spoke. In Jonas's family, you didn't question decisions—especially not the father's. Yet this time, the silence held something else: a shared sense of wonder. In that moment, Jonas glimpsed a crack in the armor, a proof that even the hardest surfaces could give way to something tender.

As they turned back toward the shelter, Jonas allowed himself to wonder—just for a moment—if there might be more tenderness hidden inside his father than he had ever dared to hope. Even as he remained dependent on the shelter and safety his family provided, he was beginning to understand that emotional closeness might be something different—something rarer. The moment itself was enough: a small, luminous truth that would live quietly in Jonas's heart.

*
**

The next day, still carrying that small luminous truth, Jonas asked his father if he might want to play tennis with him that coming Saturday morning. It wasn't a sport they had ever played together, but Jonas had recently taken a liking to it— there was something satisfying in the rhythm of the game, the back-and-forth that felt, in some small way, like a conversation.

To his surprise, his father said yes. No hesitation. Just a simple nod and the words, "Sure. Let's do it."

Jonas lay awake longer than usual that Friday night, not out of excitement, but curiosity—testing a new theory he hadn't yet put words to.

Saturday morning came, and with it, a light drizzle. Barely a mist. Jonas rose early anyway, dressed in his play clothes, and checked the court down the block—it was wet, but not unplayable. He even considered the light rain as a variable—perhaps they'd find something else to do. If the connection was real, it wouldn't depend on the weather.

He stepped quietly into his parents' bedroom. His father was still in bed, the gray morning light filtering through the blinds. Jonas asked gently, "Do you still want to play?"

His father didn't look at him when he answered.

"It's raining," he muttered. "We're not playing tennis in the rain."

There was no warmth in his voice—just a flick of dismissal. As if the whole idea had been ridiculous from the start. As if Jonas should've known better.

No alternate plan. No sign of regret. No acknowledgment of the boy who had woken early, ready not just to play—but to test a possibility.

Jonas stood there a moment longer, studying his father's face. Then he nodded once, saying only, "Okay."

It wasn't a betrayal—just a quiet data point. One more piece forming an understanding of what could and could not be counted on.

*
**

In the quiet companionship of Cecil, Jonas discovered something pure: belonging without expectation—a bond that asked nothing of him but his presence. It was a revelation that would echo gently through the years that followed, as parakeets, ducklings, hamsters, and a turtle named Turt joined his world. Each offered their own kind of refuge, a soft resistance to the silent competitions and shifting alliances he had experienced so far in his young relationships—and a reminder that while much of what he had encountered in people leaned toward performance and uncertainty, there might still be deeper, truer connections awaiting him.

But animals, as steady and forgiving as they were, couldn't answer the quiet questions Jonas had begun to carry —about what it might feel like to be met by another human being, and truly seen.

*
**

Jonas's friendships during these years revealed deeper truths about connection and disconnection. His friendship with a boy named Evan had once seemed effortless—sparked by a chance meeting while exploring the creek between their streets, where they bonded over minnows and starlight. They became summer friends first, drawn together by curiosity about the natural world, the stars overhead, and the creatures below. That friendship extended into the school year—fishing trips, tree climbing, shared adventures. One afternoon, Evan's mother suggested they take a "quiz" she would administer at their dining room table, presenting it as a fun way to learn more about themselves and each other. Jonas, drawn in innocently without any sense of competition, agreed without hesitation. Only after the papers were gathered and scored did he learn it had been an IQ test all along—a quiet reminder that in the world of grown-ups, what was presented as discovery often masked the machinery of measurement.

But subtle fractures appeared. It happened in a glance— small, but sharp enough to leave a mark. After the quiz was finished and the scores revealed, Jonas caught a different look in Evan's mother's eyes—something he couldn't fully name. Perhaps it was surprise, or perhaps it was something more cautious, as if she were searching for an explanation she hadn't expected to need. Jonas didn't understand it at the time, but he felt the shift all the same: a small, invisible distance opening between them.

So, for the time being, he accepted the unease the way one accepts a stone in their shoe—small enough to walk with, but never fully forgotten.

Over time, Jonas began to notice quiet differences between them—small at first, but growing clearer with each passing season. Evan was drawn to a different kind of competition— one rooted not in games, but in knowledge and possessions.

Evan became fascinated with grand subjects like famous maritime disasters, memorizing every detail of the Titanic's voyage, and later with expensive stereo equipment—more enamored with the gear itself than the music it could play. Impressing others with what he knew and what he owned seemed to replace the simple wonder they had once shared.

While there were still adventurous moments with Evan and others, Jonas began to recognize a pattern unfolding around him—one that shaped not just his own friendships but the friendships of those around him. Some relationships grew even stronger, fueled by shared values around competition, possessions, and popularity. It wasn't a matter of right or wrong, he realized, but of resonance—and he was beginning to see that where values aligned, friendships flourished, and where they diverged, distance quietly grew. Two boys Jonas once thought inseparable from him on the playground grew increasingly absorbed in sports and achievements. Football scores became their language, and bicycles their status symbols—not for the joy of the ride, but for the trophies of speed, brand, and shine. Jonas could appreciate their passion, but he could not summon it for things alone. His heart leaned toward adventure, discovery, the open-ended wonder of whittling tiny boats from storm-soaked wood and racing them down the rushing gutters after a summer rain. He wished they could have held onto that wonder together, but paths were diverging.

He understood that loneliness could visit anyone who lost their way from another. But Jonas had been given a different kind of compass long ago—a voice he could still hear if he listened closely, like music beneath the music, a current beneath the water. With that presence always near, even solitude felt like a kind of belonging.

Still, he wondered, if someday he found a true companion —someone whose heart beat to a rhythm closer to his own— whether losing such a bond might carry a different kind of loneliness, one he had not yet known.

Jonas was beginning to understand that belonging at the cost of himself was no belonging at all. If he was to find true allies, they would have to be those who valued presence over performance—and if not, he was willing to wait.

Beyond schoolyards and shifting friendships, another kind of belonging was being offered—one wrapped in certainty, salvation, and the promise of unconditional acceptance. And so, Jonas found himself in a youth group connected to the family's church—a new circle, a quiet promise, and an invitation unlike any he'd known.

One warm afternoon, the group piled into boats and sailed to Caladesi Island. Standing under the brilliant Florida sun, Jonas listened carefully as the youth pastor spoke of the promises of faith: a deeper sense of purpose, a joy that would reshape the heart, a community that would offer unconditional belonging.

Jonas could understand why those promises might appeal to someone—especially someone searching for meaning or a sense of safety. It was easy to see why many were drawn to those kinds of promises.

And yet, a question lingered in his mind: if salvation was so vital, why weren't his own parents—steady, pragmatic, and agnostic by their own quiet admission—more concerned? Was this another place where the Echo invited people to adopt ready-made answers because "they say" it's the right thing to do? Still, Jonas felt a responsibility to the possibility.

Perhaps stepping forward was not just about himself, but about honoring a truth his parents might have overlooked. Maybe, in some small way, it was a chance to be of service even to them.

When the pastor invited the group to declare their conversion to Christianity, Jonas looked at Evan, shrugged gently, and stepped forward.

Later, standing alone among the scrub pines and salt air,

Jonas waited for the transformation he had been promised. It never came. No overwhelming presence, no heavenly Voice. Just the same steady current he had always carried inside him —his own unnameable truth, flowing quiet and sure. He found himself wondering—what if the promised truth I'd been waiting for was actually what had been with me the whole time?

He continued to attend the youth group for a time, enjoying the fellowship, but the experience left a lasting imprint. He had a sense, even then, that organized religion might not be the center of his world. The Voice he trusted spoke in quieter, more personal tones—steady, patient, and asking nothing but that he keep listening.

At home, the Echo's lessons arrived in subtler ways.

Sometimes Jonas's parents would set up informal contests between him and his sisters—races to see who could complete the times tables first. It was presented lightly, almost playfully, a way to make learning fun.

Jonas understood even then that they meant well. But something in him noticed the deeper current beneath the game: the real reward wasn't in understanding the tables—it was in finishing first. Mastery of knowledge had given way to the urgency of being first.

His sisters seemed to love the contests, and while Jonas could never be certain what lived inside their hearts, their teasing afterward made it clear: winning was the point. Not the knowledge. Not the journey. Just the finish line.

Jonas was younger than his sisters—knew he was at a disadvantage. What stayed with him was they were showing him—how quickly warmth could cool when the spotlight moved, how easily affection could get tangled in the urge to win. Even kindness, he noticed, could shift when performance was involved.

He completed the exercises dutifully but quietly made a decision of his own. Understanding was his prize—not speed, not victory. Even if no one noticed. Even if it didn't win applause. He would measure his worth by something quieter, something truer.

And even as Jonas quietly rewrote his definition of worth, something more vulnerable was unfolding—not in games or grades, but in the quiet pull of a girl named Maria.

*
**

She lived down the street, and their families' carpools meant endless hours together, navigating the shared rhythms of school days and summers. Most afternoons, they'd wait together under the old tree outside the school, sitting in the warm hush between class and pickup. Sometimes, Jonas would get his trumpet out and play quietly while they waited. Maria would listen, watching him with soft eyes, and smile when he looked up from the music and caught her gaze. It made his heart flutter in a way he didn't yet have words for. Maria was the most beautiful girl Jonas had ever seen, a vision that made him shy, clumsy, and reverent all at once.

The local lumberyard backed up to her house, offering endless opportunities for adventure—like chasing lizards among the stacks. One afternoon, playing there, Maria asked Jonas to lie down on one of the stacks, resting his head to the side—a simple act of trust. When she kissed his cheek, Jonas body froze before his heart could respond. Instead of welcoming a moment he'd longed for, he pulled away, confused and afraid of feelings he couldn't yet name.

The friendship survived, but something delicate was lost that day.

Later, Jonas would understand: it wasn't tenderness itself that was fragile—it was the courage it took to express it. Maria had offered him a gift, and without meaning to, he had broken the trust that came with it. His heart had never turned away from her, only his fear had.

Over the years that followed, Jonas observed with quiet

sorrow how Maria's beauty, paired with her quietness, seemed to draw the wrong kind of attention—the kind who praised her beauty, pursued her with intensity, and then vanished once the chase was over. He saw how the world could reward the bold and overlook the brave, how tenderness unguarded could be mistaken for weakness.

But Jonas never forgot her, nor the lesson she had taught him without ever meaning to: that the offering of the heart is an act of profound bravery—and that it deserves a courage in return, one he vowed to someday find within himself.

*
**

By the time he reached sixth grade, Jonas had already learned how to find the rare adults who could truly see him—not just for what he achieved, but for who he was becoming. Over the years, there would be others: a neighbor who offered unexpected kindness, a camera store owner who noticed Jonas's eye for capturing the world through a simple lens, a librarian who slipped him books beyond his age level, a coach who valued effort over trophies. But Mrs. Grimsley was the first.

In the classroom, she became a quiet beacon. Without ever naming it, she recognized him—his curiosity, his way of wondering differently, his quiet resistance to being shaped by others' expectations. She fed that curiosity gently, giving him room to explore without fear of ridicule or correction. In a world of shouted demands and silent comparisons, she offered something rarer: quiet encouragement that needed no applause.

Jonas would think of her fondly for years to come, a subtle reminder that sometimes, the truest allies are the ones who never claim the title—the ones who simply stay steady, shining like a lighthouse until you are ready to find your own way.

*
**

Jonas had begun to wonder, in those years, if anyone else walked to a rhythm like his. Not adults who encouraged him quietly. Not animals who asked nothing of him. But someone —another boy—who didn't just endure the world differently, but recognized something different in him too.

He didn't know it yet, but he was about to meet that boy.

It wasn't a graceful beginning. Tommy was older, sharp-edged, and quick to judge. The first time he saw Jonas at a junior high band rehearsal, he'd written him off with a glance. Another misfit, too soft, too polished—someone to avoid. But that impression wouldn't last long.

A few weeks later, on a youth group trip, the group

bedded down on the floor of a borrowed church. Jonas had recently broken his collarbone—an accident that put him in a tightly fitting brace and left him moving stiffly. Still, he quietly kept doing what needed to be done without complaint. Lining himself up with a sleeping bag, he let his body fall backward into it with a soft thud. He didn't complain. Didn't explain. Just did what he had to do. Tommy saw it happen from across the room. And in that single moment, something shifted in him. A misjudgment fell away. A quiet respect settled in.

It didn't start with a handshake or a long talk. It started in silence—in the kind of silence that happens when someone finally sees you clearly and chooses not to walk away.

Later that night, Tommy wandered over and asked, "How'd you break the collarbone? Tree fall?"

Jonas shook his head. "Water-skiing. I wasn't supposed to be out. Said I was playing Frisbee. Parents couldn't be reached. Doctors had to wait. I had time to come up with a story."

Tommy raised an eyebrow but didn't press.

"I didn't lie just to deceive them," Jonas added after a beat. "I just didn't want to lose the freedom to keep doing things that mattered to me."

Tommy nodded. That made sense.

What followed wasn't perfect. They were still boys, after all. But it was real: camping trips patched together from scrap, ski stunts that almost got them killed, moonlit boat rides that made them laugh until they couldn't breathe. And through it all, Jonas learned something he hadn't known was possible—what it meant to have someone at your back who didn't need anything explained. He wouldn't have called it brotherhood at the time. But that's what it became.

The experiences of these years taught Jonas that belonging was not something to be won through competition, secured through conformity, or guaranteed by any promised path. It was something quieter, deeper—something that could only grow where presence was valued over performance, where the Voice within was trusted above the voices without. True belonging, he realized, would not require him to become someone else. It would ask only that he remain faithful to who he already was, even if it meant walking alone for a time.

Chapter 5 – Mischief With Purpose

The knock on Cora's window always meant one thing: mischief was afoot. But it wasn't the kind you'd find in a Saturday morning cartoon—no pie-in-the-face pranks or whoopee cushions. This mischief started after curfew, when the rest of the neighborhood was sleeping. When Jonas came calling, it was quieter, stranger. A kind of rebellion with an artist's hand. Cora never said no. Not once. Even when she knew it might end in trouble.

They were kids on the edge of something, testing fences that no one else seemed to see.

Jonas's mischief, Cora would later say, had purpose. Not to provoke for the sake of it, but to breathe, to move, to stay alive. It was like watching someone tap on the walls of a maze to make sure they were still there.

*
**

Cora's family lived next door in a multi-generational household: her father, a brilliant man who worked on secret government contracts for the Defense Department; her mother, a civic-minded woman active in local politics and worthy causes; her sister; and her grandmother—the silent observer who saw what others refused to see.

It was the grandmother who first raised the alarm. Her bedroom window faced Jonas's house, close enough to hear everything. She didn't flinch at swearing in general—she was from a tough generation—but something about Jonas's father's voice chilled her.

"Lots of people swear," she once said. "Doesn't bother me. But that man? That man swears and it terrifies me."

She said it like a confession, low and quiet. There were nights when she heard shouting—God damn it, Jonas!—followed by thuds that made her body tighten. Cora remembered those nights too. "He felt like a bomb," she once told Jonas. "A bomb with a lit fuse."

*
**

The grandmother had once considered calling child protective services. But the thought lived in the shadows of her mind, never fully stepping into daylight. She came from an era where you didn't interfere. You prayed. You hoped. You listened.

The sense of danger her grandmother felt didn't seem to reach the others—not clearly, not then. Cora's father, who liked Jonas but disliked his father, may have suspected more than he admitted. She believed now that he was probably scared of the man.

Cora herself hadn't always known what she was witnessing. But when she didn't have the words, she'd touch her fingertips to her lips—a silent acknowledgment that something mattered. She always remembered how Jonas looked at his father—not with fear, but with a kind of scientific curiosity, like a researcher watching a volatile element in a lab. She called that bravery.

*
**

It was summertime. The school year had emptied out behind them, and the long-anticipated church trip to Gatlinburg was set to begin that evening. Excitement had been building for days—Cora, Thomas, and Rachel were all going, and for a while that summer, it felt like everything was pointed toward the mountains.

That night, Cora's parents hosted a small get-together with friends—grown-ups on the porch, music drifting low, and a half-watched cooler of drinks in the kitchen. The adults weren't careless, just distracted. Cora and her sister helped themselves to a splash of rum—just enough to feel a spark— but Jonas took more. He mixed it with Gatorade like it was a science project, then drank until the room began to tilt.

Cora noticed first. She pulled Rachel and Thomas aside. "Heads up, you guys," she said quietly. "Jonas is drunk. What are we gonna do?"

They did what people always do with a drunk friend— walked him around the block, handed him water, tried everything they could think of to keep him from facing what they all feared most: his father. But time was running out, and the church bus would be arriving any minute.

Thomas thought it best to let things slide—what Dad didn't know wouldn't set him off. "He's not exactly the sentimental type," he muttered.

But Rachel wouldn't have it. Whether out of principle or spite, no one could tell. Maybe it was the slap—or the punch that came back—that stirred something sharp in her. She'd been oddly entertained by Thomas's efforts to slap Jonas into clarity, and had taken a turn herself. Jonas, reflexive and confused, had responded with a punch to her neck. It wasn't hard, but it was enough.

"You have to say goodbye to Dad," she said, like it was law. "It's weird if you don't." In the end, Rachel won out—and Thomas, resigned, took on the job.

From Cora's front yard, they crossed the quiet strip of lawn that separated the two houses, passed through the front door of Jonas's house, and made their way through the living room where the only light came from the flickering blue of the television. Thomas propped Jonas up like a doll in the master bedroom doorway, trying to make it look like nothing was wrong.

"Bye, Dad!" Jonas chirped, slurring cheerfully.

"What's wrong with you? Have you been drinking?"

He moved like lightning and for a second, it looked like he might strike Thomas. He stepped forward, right up into the boy's face, and hissed "get the hell out of my house." But Thomas didn't flinch. He locked eyes with him—steady, unblinking—and said, "I was just trying to help sir."

The old man turned and in the next breath, Jonas was yanked through the house, his shirt twisted in a fist, then flung onto his own bed like a sack of dirty laundry. The door slammed with a thunderclap.

***

Jonas woke around midnight, the room dark and still. For a moment, he lay there, confused—his head heavy, his mouth dry, and his limbs slow to obey. Then he sat up. The house was silent. He was in his bed. And the bus to Gatlinburg? Gone.

The memory didn't come back all at once, but it didn't have to. He remembered the rum. He remembered the slaps. He remembered the door slamming shut.

That's when it hit him—he'd been left behind. But he wasn't going to let that be the story.

He moved quietly, grabbing his sock full of crumpled bills —money from lawns mowed, pools skimmed. Then he slipped out of the house and headed to the Greyhound station, where he handed over the cash without flinching. "One ticket to Gatlinburg please."

The ride took 25 hours. Through the southern night and into the mountains, he sat thinking. Not about fear, not about punishment. He knew his father wouldn't react immediately. This was the kind of offense where the old man's rage slowed, turned inward, calculating.

So when Jonas arrived in Gatlinburg, he would make the call—not to prove anything, but to keep his mother from worrying. His father's only response would be, "Hmm. That's interesting." Jonas would tell his mom he loved her and hang up. The reckoning would come, but not today.

The Greyhound didn't take him all the way. It stopped in Pigeon Forge, five miles short of the final destination. From there, Jonas climbed onto an ancient school bus—no windows, no air, just the drone of the engine and a driver who looked half-mad, humming to himself. The road was narrow and steep, winding through the mountains with nothing but space beyond the shoulder.

Jonas stared out at the trees, gripping the metal bar in front of him, smiling. This was his decision. His way. And it looked like he might actually make it.

Around 3 o'clock, the bus rolled into Gatlinburg. Downtown was buzzing with people. Jonas hoisted his suitcase and started walking, hoping to spot someone he knew. And then—

"Oh my God, there's Jonas!"

Thomas's voice. Up the hill. Running feet.

Jonas turned and smiled as his friends ran toward him, mouths open in disbelief.

"How the hell did you get here?"

Jonas just shrugged. "Took the scenic route."

The rest of the trip was everything they'd hoped for— shared jokes, stolen moments, and the wide-open feeling that only comes from being far from home. On the ride back, Jonas sat quietly by the window, watching the trees blur past, wondering when the reckoning would come.

But the reckoning never came. Jonas could only guess why. Maybe his mother saw the look on his father's face—

heard that single, measured response—and gently suggested he let it go. Or maybe, for once, his father had been quietly impressed. Or maybe it was both. Either way, Jonas had slipped through untouched. Again.

After that, something changed. Jonas didn't become a leader or a symbol—most kids still played by the rules, clinging to the script. But for a few— Cora, Thomas—the ripple ran deeper. What he did lingered in the air around them, not as an example to follow, but as a question that might never be answered: What does it mean when someone breaks the rules... and the people in charge don't punish them?

*
**

That summer, the mischief started to split—some of it lighthearted, some of it flirting with real risk. Things like taking their family cars on late-night joyrides. Like the night Jonas and Cora got stuck on the roof when his parents came home early. Or the back porch scramble—half a dozen neighborhood kids gathered on Jonas's patio, goofing off until the front door slammed. Everyone scattered. Birds flapped. One kid, Randall, yelled 'crawl!' while Cora tripped over the table trying to escape. Even the neighbors knew to fear that man.

Each story became legend. But they weren't just antics. They were dispatches—unspoken messages, smuggled out through action—from kids trying to carve out airspace in a sometimes suffocating world.

*
**

When things felt heavy, Jonas and Cora went to the beach. They'd drag the seine net through shallow water, catch fish, and stock Cora's saltwater aquarium. Then they'd watch for hours—eyes tracking gills and fins like scientists and poets. Cora said later that the ocean, animals, and nature had saved her. Jonas understood. The natural world didn't demand performance. It didn't yell.

What they didn't know yet was that years later, the stories would begin to shift. People would soften the edges, smooth over what had once been sharp. Rachel, for one, would start painting a different picture of their father.

"He was just a funny old man," she'd say, as if she'd grown up in a different house altogether.

But Cora would never buy the revisions. She would tell Jonas quietly, "He didn't hit her. But I knew he hit you. I will never unhear the tone in his voice. The way it would even scare my grandmother."

Cora wouldn't rewrite the past—because she wouldn't

need to. In a world where even family might shape memory for comfort, she would become something else entirely: a keeper of the unsanitized truth. Jonas wouldn't fully understand that until much later—but something in him already knew it mattered.

But for now, the mischief remained real. It lingered—but so did something else. For Jonas, mischief wasn't an act of defiance. It was survival.

He didn't rebel in the usual ways...

He didn't fit the mold. But he moved. He acted. He found escape routes, turned mischief into meaning.

Cora would later say she was impressed—and horrified—that he never changed his behavior, even when it got him in trouble. It was never about testing rules for fun. It was about staying himself, in a house that demanded silence.

To Cora, that made him brave.

To Jonas, it was just tapping on the walls—his way of knowing he was still there.

Chapter 6 – Risk and Reward

Jonas's first two years at public high school were shaped by the logistical chaos of an overcrowded system. With the school operating on split sessions to accommodate too many students, upperclassmen attended early mornings while underclassmen filled the afternoon slots. Jonas, academically advanced, was scheduled for classes in both sessions—an exhausting, joyless stretch from dawn to dusk. The long days left little room for curiosity or creativity, and his grades began to suffer. His teachers saw potential; his report cards told a different story. It was clear early on that the system wasn't built for boys like Jonas—restless, bright, and hungry for something more than routine. In the meantime, he created his own version of school—one where the risks were real, and the lessons came with salt water and freedom.

*
**

That "something more" began with a borrowed afternoon and an old motorboat parked in the grass beside the driveway. Thomas—who was a few years older, with a car and a driver's license—began the experiments with Jonas there, timing their outings to the hour, always making sure to return the boat before the grown-ups arrived home from work. The trick was in the details: backing the trailer into the exact brown tire spots in the lawn, resetting the blocks, brushing the grass just enough to make it look untouched. They got good at it. It wasn't just the thrill of getting away with it—it was the satisfaction of putting everything back so perfectly that no one ever suspected a thing.

But not every day went smoothly. One afternoon, after putting the boat back in the yard and removing all traces, Jonas and Thomas were sitting in the grass talking about the day, when Jonas's father pulled into the driveway—earlier than expected. The boys kept their cool, greeted him with casual hellos, and exchanged a few words. It seemed they were in the clear. But just moments later, Jonas's father came back out and asked Thomas if he had a metric socket wrench in his toolbox. Thomas, thinking fast, said sure, and headed to his car. As he popped the trunk, his eyes landed on the day's giveaway: all the ski equipment from their trip, piled in plain sight. He slammed the trunk shut just in time and turned around, calling back over his shoulder that the toolbox wasn't in the trunk after all. Jonas's father, only steps behind, raised an eyebrow but said nothing more. It was a narrow escape—

and one they wouldn't forget.

Eventually, the motorboat was moved to a high-and-dry marina down on the Intracoastal Waterway, and the risk calculus changed. Now it was as simple as showing up and asking for the boat. Still, Jonas understood instinctively that he was entering a place—and a time—where he didn't belong. Any adult at the marina could recognize that a teenager appearing in the middle of a school day was cutting class—there was no hiding that. So instead of pretending otherwise, Jonas chose honesty—but paired it with respect. He didn't lie, he didn't brag, and when needed, he even asked for discretion outright. He believed that trust wasn't something you could assume; it had to be earned. That meant remembering names, introducing himself and Thomas by name, and treating the marina community like real people—not obstacles to navigate. He wasn't trying to charm anyone; he was trying to be seen as trustworthy. And it worked. The secret to bending rules, it turned out, was being responsible with the truth, and making people feel like they were part of the story, not outside of it.

Over time, the marina no longer felt like forbidden ground. It felt like something he'd earned. And with that familiarity came the courage to try something bigger. The sailboat.

*
**

By the time Jonas began taking the family sailboat out alone, he already had a blueprint for how to manage risk. The marina environment had become familiar territory—he knew who to greet, who to avoid, and how to leave as little trace as possible. But sailing was a different beast than the motorboat. It wasn't just about sneaking in and out unnoticed—it was about mastering the elements. The boat itself was larger, more complicated, and, in the eyes of his father, an extension of himself—precise, demanding, and not to be disturbed.

Unlike the rigid outings of his childhood, where everything had to be just so—sails trimmed perfectly, headings precise, no room for error—Jonas sailed for the feeling of it. The quiet rush of cutting through the water under wind alone, the dolphins riding the bow wave, the wheeling seabirds overhead. For Jonas, it wasn't about performance—it was about presence and a belonging within nature.

He'd take the boat out for entire afternoons, taking it it from its slip at the marina and disappearing into the bay, sometimes all the way to the Gulf. Every trip was a careful operation: halyards and sheets had to be reset exactly as they were found; mooring lines tied just right, padlock oriented in the correct direction. His father would notice if anything was out of place. Jonas knew this.

He carried a Polaroid camera and developed a system—photos of rigging details before setting sail, snapshots of locker arrangements and hatch orientation. It wasn't paranoia. It was preservation. The cost of discovery would be far greater with the sailboat than with the motorboat. But the reward—the full-body, full-soul sensation of gliding under open sky—was worth it every time.

*
**

Amidst the water-soaked afternoons and high-stakes escapes, something softer began to bloom—unexpected, magnetic, and new. Her name was Paige. She was smart, poised, and just mischievous enough to see something familiar in Jonas's eyes. They first met in the hallway of their tenth-grade year—Paige with damp hair from gym class and that unmistakable light in her eyes—a moment that stayed with Jonas, even as their connection deepened through the warmth of a local Christian youth group—a social hub of skating nights, potluck dinners, and living room dance parties that created a sense of belonging Jonas hadn't realized he was missing.

Paige's home was a magnet for all of it. Her parents were welcoming and kind, creating the kind of household where everyone felt safe, where the lights were always on and the fridge never empty. She had an older sister—a little wilder, a lot of fun—and the older teens in Paige's orbit brought energy and stories that widened Jonas's world. He found himself drawn not just to Paige, but to the entire environment she embodied: one of connection, care, and consistency.

Paige grounded Jonas in a way that sailing couldn't. She made him laugh, challenged the quiet distance he kept from most people, and brought out a sweetness he didn't show many people. He opened up to her slowly but fully—letting her in on the thrill of his secret adventures, even showing her the Polaroids he used to cover his tracks. For Jonas, it wasn't just a crush. It was his first real experience of emotional intimacy.

Though they shared time in the youth group, Paige's faith ran deeper than Jonas's curiosity. She was a genuine believer —gentle but certain. Jonas, ever the observer, measured it from a distance. He didn't dismiss it, but neither did he embrace it. And yet, that difference never got in the way of their early affection.

Even as they grew closer, there was something quietly bittersweet about it. Paige's life was orderly, aspirational, and firmly rooted in the world Jonas had already begun slipping away from. She embodied The Echo—graceful, well-liked, and deeply aligned with the norms that shaped her world. But none of that mattered to Jonas in those early moments. All he knew was how she made him feel: seen, wanted, hopeful.

He didn't yet know that their story would be interrupted —that he'd be sent away without warning, and that Paige, as loyal as she was to the idea of Jonas, wouldn't be able to reach across the distance. For now, it was spring, and the sun was on their faces, and she was laughing at something he'd said. And for the first time in a long time, Jonas wasn't trying to get away. He was trying to stay.

*
**

That desire to stay—to be seen, to belong—wasn't just about Paige. It was part of something larger, a pattern still forming beneath the choices he was learning to make. He was learning how to navigate risk—not just the physical risks of skipping school or borrowing boats, but the emotional ones: trusting someone, showing himself, letting people in. With each escape, each close call, and each quiet conversation with Paige, Jonas was sharpening a skill that would shape the rest of his life. He was learning how to walk the line between what the world expected and what his spirit needed. And more than that—he was beginning to understand the cost of freedom, and the courage it would take to keep choosing it. Not the kind of freedom that was promised by fitting in or following the path laid out for him, but the quieter kind—claimed moment by moment, on his own terms, guided by something deeper than approval.

Chapter 7 – Exile and Discovery

Jonas didn't know where they were going when his parents loaded him into the car one spring morning near the start of his junior year. No discussion, no warning, just motion— quiet, heavy, determined. The silence in the car said everything. When the gates of Griffin Academy appeared on the horizon, it clicked. They were leaving him there, in a place chosen to solve a problem, the slipping grades. No dialogue, no curiosity—just a decision they believed would separate him from the world they saw as the source of the problem.

They filled out some paperwork, said something brief—for Jonas, forgettable—and drove away. There was no ceremony, no long goodbye. Just a quiet departure that, at the time, Jonas couldn't fully name. He wondered later if they'd avoided warning him because they thought he'd try to run. But the truth was, if he'd really wanted to escape, the school gates wouldn't have stopped him. The whole thing, in hindsight, felt oddly theatrical—like trying to escape the weather by changing your mailing address.

*
**

At the time, Jonas didn't quite know what he felt. It wasn't abandonment, exactly. More like exile—an emotional dislocation more than a logistical one. The Academy was far from home in every sense, including Thomas and Paige. The students were foreign in culture and in manner. Children of diplomats and businessmen from Europe, the Middle East, and South America, many had grown up together in this rarefied bubble. Jonas, the newcomer from a modest Southern town, was a stranger with no map.

He tried calling home once from the pay-phone in the dorms—the way the rich kids made calls, and how everyone received inbound ones. The long-distance operator placed a collect call to his parents. The answer came back simple and flat: charges not accepted. That was the whole call. They didn't even ask why he was calling. Jonas hung up and smiled faintly, unsurprised. His father was being entirely true to form —consistent, predictable, and uninterested in deviation. There was something strangely affirming about that. When reality confirms your expectations, it gives you a kind of certainty. And that certainty, he realized, could be a kind of comfort, even if it stung a little.

Jonas was already aware of a quiet kind of freedom in the situation. No one to report to. No one to correct him. No father's eyes following him from room to room. The Academy still had rules, yes—but they were institutional, not personal. He wasn't being judged by someone's mood or some unspoken moral code. The Academy's rules were more like curbs on a road—there to keep everyone heading the same direction, not to punish you for how you drove. Within those lines, Jonas found a surprising kind of autonomy. He could feel the shape of his own days beginning to form, and the feeling sent a quiet thrill through him.

But structure wasn't the only thing that marked the divide. What truly defined the distance between Jonas and the others was something less visible—until it wasn't.

*
**

It was the difference in means that struck him first. Jonas had fifteen dollars a week—enough for a few meals in town or a secondhand record. But other students carried three hundred, sometimes more. They ordered pizza delivered to campus, bought designer clothes, cars and took weekend trips like it was nothing. It wasn't just wealth—it was the ease, the casual fluency in privilege. Jonas had seen plenty of that in movies and on television, but to witness it so fully formed, so natural in a community this small—it caught him off guard.

He noticed early on how that wealth shaped everything,

especially attraction. There were just under 230 students on campus. Maybe sixty of them were American, and fewer than half were girls. A good number of the American girls gravitated toward the boys who had the most to spend, regardless of where they came from. Jonas could see it without judgment, just a kind of quiet fascination. It made a strange kind of sense. For kids raised around power and money, it was familiar, magnetic. But it also made him a little sad. There didn't seem to be much room left for the softer sparks—those quiet, personal attractions built on shared glances, curious minds, or the feeling of being truly seen. Just gravity pulling everyone toward the same gold center.

*
**

When people felt unreachable, Jonas turned toward something quieter, something familiar.

At first, he ate alone. He wandered the campus like a quiet observer, studying from the edges. He found unexpected comfort at the stables. The Academy had an equestrian program—a natural fit for its well-heeled student body—and though Jonas didn't ride, he found himself drawn to the horses. He'd stand near the fences, talk to them when no one else was around, soaking in their steady, grounded energy. Animals had always made more sense than people, and while these horses were bigger than any of the animals in his life so far, their size didn't matter—it was their quiet presence, their steady way of being that comforted him.

There was a particular American girl he noticed often, brushing down a tall chestnut mare. She had a natural ease with the animal and a quiet beauty Jonas couldn't help but admire. He thought about starting a conversation, asking something about the horse—but something about her polished confidence gave him pause. She seemed completely at ease in this world, and Jonas wasn't sure he was ready to cross that space. Part of him still felt tethered to Paige, anyway—and the idea of stepping outside that connection, even slightly, didn't feel right.

*
**

Jonas was already becoming fluent in the subtleties of eye contact. Some looks were invitations. Others were dismissals. Hers was neither. She did look his way, now and then—but not as an invitation. It was more like a nod from a stage to an audience: she saw that he saw her, and that seemed to please her. Jonas was learning the language of looks—how beauty and wealth could confer a kind of quiet power. This girl wore that power with ease, like something she inherited. Being noticed confirmed something she already believed. And Jonas, careful not to mistake that moment of affirmation for an invitation, simply took note. He understood. In this new world, attention moved along different currents. And so did Jonas.

And then there was Tali, an American girl raised in the Caribbean who shared his growing love for 70s folk and rock music. She was beautiful too—but different. Not polished or performative. Tali wasn't interested in being noticed; she was interested in noticing. She asked questions, listened with her whole face, and led with her heart. They talked music, swapped albums, sat in the sun with guitars and stories.

Tali was fully at ease in this world of privilege—she'd grown up with it—but what made her rare was that she didn't rely on it. Her comfort wasn't rooted in status. And her openness gave Jonas something he hadn't found yet: a way to move through this world without feeling like an intruder. With her, he began to find something he hadn't felt in a long time: ease. And slowly, Jonas began to feel the ground beneath him again.

*
**

But even with friendship blooming and music in the air, the Academy had its darker corners.

Some things couldn't be seen from the glossy brochures or polite campus tours. One of them was the blanket party tradition. It was a kind of hazing, mostly carried out by the older boys—late at night, they'd sneak into a new student's room, throw a blanket over his head, and deliver a flurry of punches and kicks in the dark.

It wasn't personal. That was what made it worse. Jonas had grown up knowing exactly what personal bullying felt like—being chased through the neighborhood, mocked in the church hallway, made to feel like he didn't belong by people who knew his name. This was different. It wasn't about him— it was about the role he'd been assigned as "the new kid." That kind of anonymity, the randomness of it, gave it a colder edge. You couldn't prepare for it by being nicer or smarter. You could only brace for it.

And Jonas did.

*
**

The older boys weren't exactly subtle about it. There were too many sidelong glances, snickers that trailed off when he entered the room, and half-whispered conversations that broke up as soon as he passed by. It was all just obvious enough to be careless—and Jonas, ever the observer, picked up on it. They didn't seem to realize he was watching them watch him. By Thursday, he was almost certain. "He considered his options—telling a teacher felt useless, and asking for protection would only confirm his outsider status. So he made a call. There was only one person he trusted to have his back."

On the Friday before the weekend he suspected it would happen, Thomas—his best friend from back home—drove up for a visit. Jonas let him in through a side door to the dormitory, and together they laid in wait. Sure enough, just past midnight, the boys crept in with a blanket and their bravado.

As one of them raised the blanket, Thomas stepped in fast, catching the boy's arm and landing a quick jab to his midsection—just enough to knock the wind out of him. Jonas shoved another hard enough to knock him off balance. The others froze, stunned, then scattered. They weren't expecting resistance—certainly not expecting backup.

When it was over, Jonas and Thomas laughed harder than they had in months.

It wasn't about revenge. It was about reclaiming something. In a place that had stripped him of familiarity, that night gave Jonas back a piece of himself. And with it, a deeper bond with the friend who knew who he was before all this.

After the adrenaline of that night faded, things began to

shift again—this time in a quieter, more lasting way.

Before Thomas left, the two of them stood outside the dorm in the early morning hush. No big speeches. Just a long look, a shared laugh, and a nod that said more than words could have. They both knew what that night had meant. And for Jonas, the memory of it would settle in his chest like a kind of ballast—steadying, real.

*
**

The Academy's headmaster and his wife noticed Jonas early on—not because he tried to stand out, but because he didn't. There was something quietly self-possessed about him, something steady behind the eyes. He wasn't flashy, and he clearly didn't have the resources many of the other students had. While others spent hundreds each week on food, clothes, or travel, Jonas made his fifteen dollars stretch with careful restraint and little complaint.

One afternoon, after spotting him helping younger students near the waterfront, Elsa—the headmaster's wife—called Jonas into the office. What followed wasn't discipline—it was an offer. The Academy needed a student to serve as director of waterfront activities. It was a job usually held by a senior, but Elsa said she trusted Jonas. The pay was $2.50 an hour, and she handed him something that made it feel very real: a timecard. The Academy used an old-school punch system for its student employees, and now Jonas had one of his own. That's how he would log his hours, and it was up to him to track them honestly. "Call it stewardship," Elsa had said with a smile.

Jonas took to the role immediately. The boats, the quiet rhythms of the lake, the ritual of responsibility — it all fit. He'd grown up water-skiing in the summers and felt at home near the docks. There was peace in knowing Elsa and her husband Clarence trusted him to be alone, unsupervised, and still do what needed to be done. It gave Jonas not just a job, but a place. And with it, the beginning of something he hadn't expected: belonging.

*
**

As his role near the lake settled into rhythm, the rest of campus life continued to unfold around him.

Jonas went through a few false starts when it came to roommates. One snored so loudly it was like sharing a room with a generator. Another insisted on blasting disco at all hours, and a third treated the room like a private nightclub. Eventually, though, he landed with someone who felt like a decent fit — a senior named Drew, the class president and drummer for the Academy jazz band. Drew was calm, focused, and gave Jonas room to be himself.

By then, Jonas had brought his old gut-string guitar out more often. It was a beat-up Kay classical guitar that had lived in the house for as long as Jonas could remember. No one played it, and no one ever talked about where it came from—until one day, his mother mentioned it had been bought with green stamps. Just like the bugle. But this time, it wasn't his. His parents had redeemed the stamps themselves. That small detail struck him. Something about the idea of choosing a guitar and then letting it gather dust. He picked it up because no one else had. And over time, it became his—not just in possession, but in spirit. He played it not out of tradition or training, but because it filled a space nothing else did. The trumpet, once his primary instrument, had always required fitting into a larger whole—marching bands, concert ensembles, jazz trios. But the guitar was different. It sat in his lap like it had always belonged there. It was private, portable, intimate. He started learning songs from the 70s—James Taylor, Cat Stevens, John Denver—working through chord changes alone in his room or out on the lawn with Tali.

Still, the trumpet had its place. When Drew invited him to join the school's touring jazz band, Jonas accepted. They played standards and swing charts—nothing cutting edge, but tight, clean, and well-received. The Academy took pride in the group, sending them out to perform at local schools and various events around the region as ambassadors. For the first time in his life, Jonas experienced what it meant to be celebrated for his contribution—not just tolerated or disciplined. And traveling with the band gave him a kind of sanctioned freedom. He was moving through the world under the banner of something larger, but for once, it didn't erase who he was—it amplified it.

One afternoon after a performance, the headmaster approached him privately. Without much fanfare, he handed Jonas a silver coin, custom-minted with the Academy's crest one side and the headmaster's own name and face on the other. It wasn't flashy, but Jonas understood what it meant. He kept it in his treasure box for years. Still does.

*
**

The boys' dorm had its own way of resolving conflict. When arguments couldn't be settled with words—and when the dorm parents chose to stay out of it—the television room furniture was pushed aside, and a pair of boxing gloves came out. It wasn't tradition in any formal sense, but everyone knew the drill.

Jonas had never been in a fight. He'd always relied on his words, on timing, on staying two steps ahead of tension. But this time, that wasn't enough. One of his records—an album he'd brought from home—had gone missing. Another boy claimed it was his. The story split the dorm. No one could prove anything. So out came the gloves.

Neither of them knew what they were doing. It was two boys swinging blind, hoping luck would land somewhere. And for Jonas, it did. He caught the other boy with an early, awkward jab—more surprised than strategic—and knocked him off his feet. No one was hurt. No blood, no bruises. Just a stunned pause, and then it was over.

What surprised Jonas most was what came next. The other boy stood up, nodded, and that was it. No hard feelings. In fact, they got along better afterward. Something about the fight cleared the air.

Jonas had seen this kind of thing in movies—boys becoming friends only after throwing punches, bloodied lips turning into grudging respect. He understood the trope, even if it never made much sense to him. That wasn't how he related to people—never had been. Still, here it was, playing out in real time. Only this version was more awkward than anything else—and, in its own way, more merciful. No blood. No torn shirts. Just awkward swings and a moment of strange mutual understanding—a clumsy kind of peace offering, but real nonetheless.

*
**

And just when the noise seemed to settle, love returned—in a familiar script, written in ink and hope.

Jonas and Paige tried to keep their connection alive through letters. They wrote often, their letters taking on a kind of rhythm—loops, cross-outs, little drawings in the margins. It wasn't dramatic. It was sweet. They missed each other.

Thomas had started to notice the distance wearing on Jonas. In a recent call, Jonas had admitted—quietly—that he thought Paige might be pulling away. Kate, his girlfriend and one of Paige's closest friends, had picked up on the same shift. Whether the idea came from her or from Thomas didn't matter. He took it to heart and came up with a plan.

He suggested the four of them—himself, Kate, Paige, and Jonas—go to Grad Night at Disney World, an annual celebration for high school juniors and seniors where the park stayed open late and live bands played across the grounds.

With Thomas's car, it was easy. He, Kate, and Paige made the drive from back home up to the Academy to pick up Jonas, and then the four of them continued on to Orlando— sharing stories, music, and the kind of anticipation that made the night feel like a reward.

It should've been pure magic. And for a while, it was. Jonas and Paige danced to songs they both knew, laughed on rides, slipped into old rhythms like nothing had changed.

But everything had.

By the end of the night, they both knew the truth. The distance was too much. Their lives had begun to stretch in different directions, and neither one could pull hard enough to keep the connection taut. They said goodbye—not dramatically, just with the quiet ache of letting go.

Paige eventually found someone new and dated him through the end of high school. She went on to college and kept moving forward. Jonas didn't resent her for it. He understood. Still, part of him quietly held on to the idea that maybe—someday—their paths would cross again. Not to rewrite the past. Just to acknowledge it had mattered.

*
**

Jonas might have graduated from the Academy, if not for what happened that fall.

It began as a ripple—unrest overseas, footage of protesters outside foreign embassies. The tension felt far away at first, just another thing happening on television. But for a school with an international student body, it hit much closer to home than anyone expected.

Roughly a third of the students came from nations where political unrest was rising, and emotions on campus began to boil. What started as debates turned into shouting matches, then vandalism. Windows were broken. Offices defaced. A small riot erupted one night, and the Academy lost its fragile hold on order.

By winter break, the headmaster and Elsa had already made the decision that The Academy would finish out the year, but they were uncertain whether it would reopen in the fall. They promised to let parents know by June, after the school year ended.

Jonas hadn't seen it coming. After everything—after exile, adjustment, friendship, discovery—he was once again packed up and sent home without warning. It wasn't his decision. It never had been.

But this time, he didn't return as the same boy who'd left. He was older. Wiser. Still idealistic, but not untouched. A quiet fire had been lit inside him—a growing sense that even in systems beyond your control, you could still shape how you moved through them.

And that, maybe, was its own kind of beginning. He hadn't asked for exile, but its silence revealed the early shape of who he might become.

Chapter 8 – Doors Closed, Windows Opened

The letter came at the end of June. The Academy wouldn't be reopening in the fall. What came next wasn't a discussion, but a directive.

His father stood at the edge of the kitchen, arms crossed, a stopwatch in one hand. "The Academy's not reopening," he said. "You have one minute. Christian Bible school or military academy. Pick."

It wasn't the first time Jonas had been handed a forced choice. He still remembered the third-grade band instrument ultimatum—how he'd been given 2 minutes to decide his musical fate. This was no different, just higher stakes. And he knew his father's timing was exact down to the second.

"Bible school," Jonas said, before the clock ran out. He could imagine the other path—shaved head, barked orders, a spirit crushed under regimentation. For all the contradictions he felt about faith, the Christian school seemed survivable. Silently, he was grateful. Not for the options, but for being given one.

*
**

Within weeks, he was enrolled at a small Christian high school known more than anything for its music program. Fewer than 250 students, but nationally recognized for its jazz band, chamber singers, marching band, and more. It didn't take long for Jonas to find his place—five music classes a day and a trumpet in one hand and a guitar and the other. Voice lessons. Ensemble rehearsals. Morning, noon, and sometimes into the evening.

Still, Jonas tested the boundaries. He grew a goatee, fully aware it was against the rules. He let it grow for about a month before the headmaster called him in. No lecture, just an expectant pause until Jonas nodded and agreed to shave. A quiet rebellion. Nothing more.

*
**

What surprised him most wasn't the school—it was the freedom within the structure. He became a regular soloist at the weekly student assemblies, often performing with just his guitar, and occasionally in duets with other students. He wasn't just tolerated—he was celebrated. The faculty noticed. So did a few others from outside the school. Something was taking shape around him, but Jonas wasn't looking ahead. For now, being present in the moment—in the music—was more than enough.

*
**

At the same time, Jonas was surrounded by students who wore their faith like uniforms. Some sincere, others... harder to read. He noticed the contrast between their public convictions and private behaviors. He didn't judge, but he did take note. It deepened a question that had been growing in him: What's real, and what's just performance?

Several girls caught his eye. Beautiful, charismatic, full of spirit. But when he looked closer, he wasn't sure what he was seeing. It wasn't fear that kept him at a distance—it was fog. He couldn't see through the layers of curated identity, couldn't find something solid to hold. And so he watched, wondered, and stayed untangled.

*
**

The year unfolded like a crescendo. The senior class swept competitions across the state. Jonas, often front and center, found himself once again in a place he hadn't chosen, yet somehow exactly where he needed to be. He laughed about it sometimes with Thomas, or quietly to himself.

"Praise the Lord, sweet baby Jesus," he'd whisper after another standing ovation.

He wasn't mocking. Not exactly. It was gratitude—wrapped in irony, seasoned with relief. The door had closed.

But the window… the window had flung wide open.

Chapter 9 – The Escape Route

Jonas graduated from high school with the world assuming he'd follow the traditional path—especially his parents. Jonas, still unsure of his own next steps, enrolled in the local junior college. He took a handful of general education classes—psychology, English comp, music theory—and kept his head down. His instructors noticed his aptitude and encouraged him to take the CLEP exams, a series of college-level placement tests that could earn him credit and accelerate his degree.

He did exceptionally well.

*
**

Within a few months, he had enough credits to qualify as a sophomore and received positive responses from nearly every public university in Florida. One offer stood out: a full scholarship to study music. On paper, it looked like everything he'd been working toward. It even sounded like a dream fulfilled—until Jonas looked deeper.

The program was rigid. It emphasized pedagogy, classical theory, and training to become a music teacher. There was no space for exploration, for voice. Jonas didn't want to teach. He didn't want to lecture about scales or analyze Bach until he hated him. He wanted to write. To play. To feel the music before understanding it. To chase something deeper.

And that chase had already begun.

*
**

By then, Jonas had started playing guitar and singing in local clubs and tiki bars across the county. He mostly performed popular covers from the '60s and '70s—James Taylor, Cat Stevens, Carole King—but even within the constraints of familiar songs, something stirred. He felt alive under the dim lights, mic in front of him, the subtle buzz of feedback in the air. Here, he wasn't performing to pass a class. He was becoming someone.

He thought about the scholarship. About classrooms, lesson plans, and tenure tracks. Then about the guitar in his hands, and the look on people's faces when he played a song they loved in a way they hadn't heard before. The decision came quietly but clearly: he would turn it all down.

Jonas declined the scholarship. He chose not to enroll at any university. And he hadn't told his parents yet.

*
**

That night, he couldn't sleep. He lay awake, eyes on the

ceiling, fingers laced over his stomach, listening to the hum of the fan overhead. He knew a storm would come the moment he spoke the truth aloud to his father. But still—he felt sure.

Eventually, sleep took him. And in the dream, he stood in a field of tall grass, the sky above turning from gold to indigo. The air was still. And just beyond the hill, he saw a man.

Not someone he recognized. Not exactly. But there was a sense of knowing. A feeling as old as breath. The man's presence was quiet, weathered, kind. Familiar in a way that bypassed memory and went straight to the center of him.
The man looked at him. Sadness shimmered in his eyes. Then he spoke:

"This voice you hear—never let it go."
"I made that mistake," the man whispered. "I traded truth for comfort. And it cost me everything. Please—when you hear the Echo calling, remember: the Voice is quiet. But it is real. Follow it."

Jonas felt his throat tighten. "Who are you?" he asked. "How do I know you? And what do you mean it cost you everything?" The man didn't answer. Instead, his expression softened further, and he offered only this:

"Constance has something for you."

Before Jonas could ask who Constance was, the man

turned and began walking toward the light just beyond the hill. His figure blurred, then dissolved like breath on glass.

*
**

Jonas woke just before dawn, heart pounding—not with fear, but with recognition.

The name reverberated in his mind—Constance. He didn't know who that was. Or if it even was a name. But the feeling lingered. Like something left behind on purpose.*

The escape route wasn't to a place. It was a choice.

And now, he would have to say it out loud.

Chapter 10 – The Rebellion Begins

When Jonas announced that he was dropping out of college to play music, his father didn't speak for a full minute. The silence felt heavy, pressing down on every surface, like it might break something fragile if it lasted too long. His father's hands were tight around the edge of the table, and his mother just stood there, arms folded loosely, not meeting anyone's eyes.

They had known, of course. Known about the late-night gigs and the local clubs, about how Jonas had been sitting in with older musicians, slowly building a reputation. But they hadn't said a word—not because they approved, but because they assumed it would pass. That the scholarship would anchor him. That the university would smooth out whatever wildness was still left in him. That he'd fall in line. Become a productive member of society. That illusion had now been broken.

Finally, his father spoke. "You think you can just waste everything we worked for?"

The words weren't surprising. The tone was. There was

something behind them Jonas couldn't place—like his father wasn't just talking to him, but to someone else entirely. Jonas didn't reply. His silence wasn't defiance this time—it was a gnawing question: What am I missing here?

His father's gaze drifted to the overflowing garbage can. "You can't even take out the trash. You think you're ready to be anything?"

That's when it happened. Without yelling, without threats, just a calm, brutal sentence: "Get out, before I smash your face through the wall and you won't know what hit you until you pick it up on the other side."

Jonas blinked. He searched his father's face, looking for the familiar signs—sternness, disappointment, even contempt. But what he saw was something else entirely. Like he wasn't even the one being punished.

Jonas nodded slowly. The message was clear and it had nothing to do with the trash. His father had always handled bigger offenses with unnerving calm—like the time Jonas was made to grow a garden for the entire summer as punishment for being brought home by the police after being found exploring the neighborhood barefoot at 2 am. That kind of measured response was normal.

But this—this explosion—felt different. As if his father couldn't bring himself to face the truth of what Jonas had said about college. As if the small thing gave him permission to react to the big thing. But there was something more, Jonas could feel it. A shadow behind the reaction. Something deeper he didn't understand yet—like his decision had cracked open a part of his father that had nothing to do with him. Not really.

Jonas grabbed his guitar case, slung his pack over one shoulder, and stepped into the night—one foot into exile, the other into freedom.

He needed time to figure out a plan that was certain. But right then, he needed a place to stay while he figured it out. So he walked straight to his sister Elaine's place across town. They were on good terms and she'd been coming out to watch Jonas play so she'd understand the situation. When he arrived, she opened the door in her slippers, her eyes wide but not surprised. "Come in," she said. No questions, no judgment. For a few months, her place was home. Back then, they were still close—still orbiting within a common family reality. It wouldn't last, but for a while, it mattered.

*
**

Back at his parents house, once Jonas was gone, his father muttered something about how the boy had always been a problem—too stubborn for his own good, always doing things his way. His mother didn't respond, but inwardly, she couldn't help but remember a different version of the story. She remembered all the little rebellions—signs that Jonas had never really belonged to the same mold his father came from.

She thought back to his first act of rebellion, not long after his first birthday. The day the minister tried to baptize him, little Jonas had blown a raspberry and spit right in the man's face. The congregation gasped, the minister nearly dropped him, and she could feel the heat of her husband's glare from behind her. Secretly, she'd been amused, though she wouldn't have admitted it then.

Then there was the kindergarten graduation, when his name was called to get his diploma. He just sat there, small hands in his lap, eyes fixed on some point on the floor. After calling his name three times, the teacher gave her a nervous glance, and she gave Jonas a little nudge with her elbow. He looked up at her, his brow furrowing like he was genuinely confused, and said, "I don't want it." The crowd's soft laughter only made his father's face harden with embarrassment. But she couldn't help but feel a strange pride —how many five-year-olds questioned the importance of a piece of paper?

And she couldn't forget the Sunday school incident. Jonas had been required to go, even though they themselves weren't devout Christians. But it wasn't long before the church called and asked if it might be best for him not to come back. "He just...asks too many questions," the teacher had said. His father scolded him for being disrespectful, but she couldn't help but notice how he always seemed to be looking for something more than just scripted answers—something that couldn't be memorized, only discovered.

*
**

And then there were the moments that didn't make sense to her—like the time he called from Gatlinburg, hours after missing the church bus that Cora, Rachel, Thomas, and all the others had taken. He wasn't asking permission, just letting her know he was safe. His voice had been calm, almost tender. Her husband's only response was, "Hmm. That's interesting." When Jonas got back, there was no punishment. No cold lecture. Just silence. She hadn't known what to make of it then, and she still didn't. But it stuck with her—a sharp little break in the pattern, in a household that usually had rules for everything.

Her eyes softened as her thoughts returned to Jonas. She never knew quite what to do with him, but she never really worried about him either. He wasn't trying to make trouble— he just refused to pretend that everything made sense when it didn't. In some ways, she envied him—how he didn't settle for easy explanations or just go along with things to keep the peace. Even now, as he walked away from the life his father had planned for him, she couldn't help but feel the same flicker of pride she felt at his kindergarten graduation—the same quiet admiration for his refusal to be something he wasn't.

Her husband grumbled something unintelligible, but she didn't respond. She just kept folding laundry, a small, knowing smile tugging at the corner of her mouth.

Part II: Rebel Voices in the Echo

When one voice rises, others remember how.

Songs Invitation

Songs from "The Echo and the Voice" – An Invitation

From this point in the book you will come upon fragments of lyrics for the songs written by the character, Jonas Wilder.

You're invited to bookmark the music link now, not to listen all at once, but to have it ready—so that when a song appears, you can experience it in the moment it arrives.

echoandthevoice.com/music
Music, like memory, finds us when we're ready.

Chapter 11 – The Band Forms

As warm evenings grew long and the gigs came steady, Jonas had carved out a small but loyal following in the local coffeehouses and beach side bars. It was around this time that he met Vince Crowley—a charismatic rhythm & lead guitarist with an easy smile and a knack for crowd work. What began as a spontaneous sit-in turned into something more. They clicked musically right away. Within a few months, they were performing as a duo on the local circuit, weaving harmonies and trading verses like they'd been playing together for years. Sometimes a bassist or backup vocalist would join them for a set, but mostly it was just the two of them. Easy-going, exciting, and full of possibility.

*
**

As their sound deepened and their rhythm took root, their reputation grew. The songwriting was idealistic, unpolished, and alive with purpose. Their shows began to draw larger crowds. Tips turned into paid gigs, and their names appeared on posters and chalkboards up and down the coast. There was a sense of something building. They were young, broke, and entirely convinced they were onto something that mattered.

*
**

One of the first songs Jonas began to shape in those early nights came from watching Vince struggle through a painful breakup with a longtime girlfriend he'd deeply loved. They talked about it late into the night, sometimes with guitars still in their laps, and Jonas channeled what Vince couldn't always put into words. It started as a few quiet lines scribbled in the margins of a notebook, but it stayed with them:

I'm driven by a need to do,
The things that I love most,
Aside of making love to you,
And taking walks along the coast,
I want to find out for myself,
Where I fit into this world,
And when I learn to be myself,
Then I'll learn..... to love you girl...

Even in the joy of those first gigs, the song already knew what they were still learning: that love and purpose don't always move in harmony.

*
**

The change came slowly at first—just enough to notice, then hard to ignore. The energy had started to shift. The Florida nightlife scene was seductive—sunburnt afternoons turned into neon-lit evenings, and the endless summer of bar gigs became a rhythm of its own. They'd play from 9:30 PM to 1:30 AM, hit someone's apartment for an after-hours hang, drink, smoke, sometimes get high. Crash around dawn. Sleep through the morning, roll out for volleyball or drinks on the beach, and do it all over again. It was intoxicating. And for Vince, maybe even more than the music itself.

Jonas tried to stay focused. He kept mostly sober, dodged the harder drugs, and never lost sight of why he started playing in the first place. For Jonas, music wasn't about fame. It was about clarity. Singing helped him sort the noise. Playing made him feel real. It kept him tethered to something that felt like truth. But he felt the divergence growing. What was once a shared mission was slowly becoming two different stories written on the same stage.

In the heart of all that noise and motion, Paige came back into his life.

She had graduated from university with a teaching degree and landed a job at a middle school in a nearby town. Word of Jonas's growing local fame must have reached her, because one night she appeared at the back of a crowded bar, arms folded, smiling in that half-curious, half-wistful way that said everything and nothing all at once.

Jonas had never truly let go of the idea of her. Even though he knew, deep down, they were wired differently—her world of faith, structure, and clear expectations never quite matched his—but the memory of her had never softened. They reconnected quickly. Old comfort mixed with new conversations. A quiet, tentative intimacy returned.

Paige was different. Life had touched her. Her father—once the ideal of what a man should be—had betrayed her mother and left. Paige, shaken to the core, found herself questioning everything. "If I can't trust him," she once asked Jonas, "can any man really be trusted?" That question lingered in the air whenever fans flirted with Jonas after a set—even when he remained a perfect gentleman. She wondered: Was it an act?

They shared stories. She told him about a high school boyfriend who drank too much, a college relationship that left her feeling used and discarded. Jonas thought of Maria and the boys who preyed on her innocence. He wanted to protect Paige from those memories—even if they weren't his to fix.

One night, sitting on their thrift-store couch in a dim apartment lit by a single lamp, Paige asked Jonas why he loved her. He didn't hesitate. "Because you're smart. You know what you want. You're brave enough to go after it."

She looked away and said quietly, "That's interesting. Because I'm not any of those things."

She hesitated, then gave a soft laugh. "But it makes me happy that you see me that way. Maybe I should try seeing myself more like that too."

Jonas smiled and reached for her hand. There was warmth in the moment, a flicker of hope between their uncertainties. Jonas would remember the moment as the one where he got his first real glimpse into the difference between how we are seen by others and how we see ourselves. It occurred to Jonas again later—that people carry their past into everything. Into how they see others, and into how they see themselves. Paige wasn't the only one.

Later that week, Jonas began sketching out a new song. It came out slowly—soft chords, unfinished verses. He wasn't sure if Paige would ever hear it, or even if he'd finish it, but it held something honest. A memory, reshaped by time.

The working title was "In Everything I Do."

Oh you and I could go back to the days,
When loving came so naturally.
Oh you and I should go back to the ways,
That our innocence allowed us to be.

For you I'd live and I'd die,
I love you and that's why,
There's a little bit of you in everything I do.

*
**

Within a year, they were living together. But their days rarely aligned. Paige woke up early, taught all day, and returned exhausted. Jonas was only just getting up by the time she came home, his nights just beginning as hers ended. They were like two ships passing in the night. Still, they made time for beach days, long walks, and the small rituals that kept them close.

*
**

In another year, they got married. It was a beautiful day. Families smiled, drinks flowed, and for one night the world felt harmonious. At the rehearsal dinner, Jonas heard something rare—his father belly-laughing. Not a polite chuckle, but a full, unguarded laugh. It startled him. In all his years, Jonas had never heard that sound from his father—not like that. It was jarring, almost surreal, like catching a glimpse of something wild and unguarded in a man built of restraint. Maybe it was the comfort of normalcy, or the drink, or the fact that Paige came from a family that made things look easier. Whatever it was, it softened something in the old man, if only for a moment.

Later that night, Jonas's father found him on the back deck, standing alone with a glass in hand, watching the moonlight scatter across the water. For a while, he said nothing. Then he stepped beside his son and muttered, "If I had to do it all over again, I'd do it more like you." It had been nearly five years since Jonas had told his parents he was turning down the scholarship, and his father threw him out of the house. And now, this—softer, unexpected. Jonas hoped this moment might be the start of something real, the place where repair could begin. But the words hung there, unspoken—both what had happened, and what might come next.

He didn't wait for a response. Just gave a nod, patted Jonas on the shoulder, and walked back inside.

Jonas didn't follow him. Just stood there, glass in hand, watching the back door ease shut. He wanted to believe the words meant something. Really meant something. But belief came slow when you'd built a life expecting the opposite.

Still, he noted it. Just like the time his father turned the car around at the animal shelter to go back for their cat Cecil. Or the unexpected belly laugh over dinner. These were not proof. They were flickers. The kind you file away quietly, privately—

just in case they ever add up to something you can trust.

*
**

That same year, Jonas and Vince won a local battle of the bands. The validation was electric. They packed their bags and headed for New York City, chasing the next big thing. Paige came too. She'd left her job to pursue a Master's degree, juggling classes by day and catering gigs by night. Rent was steep. Everything was steep. Jonas and Vince played wherever they could—parks, subways, coffeehouses. Sometimes even street corners.

New York wasn't waiting for them. After a few years, the dream had begun to fray. Record execs told them they were too late, too derivative. "We already have acts like this." "Try writing more like Blake Fortune or The Velvet Offset." Jonas felt the familiar frustration of being asked to become someone else. Vince, on the other hand, seemed to take it as a suggestion—not a sacrifice.

By then, Paige had finished her degree but felt done with the city—and maybe with the dream altogether. They had the conversations they'd been avoiding. Painful, but tender. She spoke about needing stability—something more like the life she'd grown up with, something rooted and real. He spoke about needing motion, risk, a kind of freedom he still didn't fully understand.

They didn't blame each other. They named the differences: faith, family, the kind of future each of them needed. They admitted they'd been best friends, lovers, anchors through uncertain years. And they admitted—just as quietly—that the thing they'd built together was no longer the thing they both needed.

They knew they'd miss each other. But they also knew what had to be done. Winter came and she went back to Florida. Maybe, in going, she was trying to become the woman he always believed her to be.

When spring arrived, they divorced. It was quiet. Inevitable. Not bitter, just heavy. Like the final note of a song that once filled the room.

What remained was the music. And a few lyrics scribbled into the margins of Jonas's notebooks—lines from songs that told the story better than he ever could.

Chapter 12 – The First Compromise

The grief didn't hit all at once. It crept in around the edges of Jonas's days—the quiet mornings, the long drives, the late nights when the audience noise faded and there was nothing left but silence. Losing Paige hadn't just ended a relationship; it had untethered something deeper.

She had been the first person he'd ever fully opened up to —the only one who knew the version of him that didn't have to perform. They'd found each other young, clung to each other through distance, and even after everything, tried to build something real. She knew the boy before the ambition. Losing her felt like losing his anchor.

But rather than wallow, Jonas did what he'd always done: he turned it into music.

The songs came in waves—semi-autobiographical, imagined, observed. He wrote about the stages of love and loss, the slippery slope from connection to estrangement. Some were wistful, others raw. *I Won't Stop Loving You, Lonely in Love with You, I Do Because I Love You, How Am I Supposed to Love Without You*. They weren't all masterpieces, but they were honest. Cathartic. And they sharpened his craft in a way it seems that only heartbreak could.

His notebook was filling with fragments—pleas, questions, half-sung confessions. One line returned again and again: *How am I supposed to love without you?* It didn't just haunt him—it guided his pen.

*
**

While Jonas mined his soul, Vince followed a different muse.

"I'm writing hits now," he said one night, tossing a beer bottle into the recycling bin like it was a declaration of war. "Stuff that actually gets us somewhere." By then, the lineup had settled. Simon Bellamy on bass, Calder Chase on drums, Jonas on rhythm guitar and vocals and David Manolis on piano. They didn't call themselves a band yet—not out loud—but they were one. Even the fights were rehearsals for something larger.

Jonas didn't argue. Vince's new songs had energy—grittier lyrics, tighter hooks. *Somewhere Between Heaven and Hell, The Original Sin, First Impressions.* They were good. And when they started folding those songs into their sets, the crowd noticed. Promoters noticed. Suddenly they were booking better gigs, longer sets, and venues beyond their hometown. The tri-state circuit started to open up like a map being unfolded. And for the first time, they were both doing fairly well financially.

But it wasn't free.

*
**

The compromises came slowly, disguised as opportunities. A promoter hinted they'd have a better shot at prime-time slots if they opened with something like "First Impressions" instead of one of their quieter songs. Vince loved it. Jonas nodded, said okay, but as the words left his mouth, he felt the sting of it—like agreeing to something he wasn't sure he believed in. Something cracked, and he knew it wasn't just the plan—it was part of himself.

*
**

Vince started playing the part—drinking more, flirting more, riding the wave like he was already famous. The chaos of it all—the women, the post-show parties, the late-night disappearances—made Jonas feel like he was watching a slow-motion derailment.

The shift in the crowd was subtle at first. Where once their music had stirred hearts and sparked reflection, now the energy seemed to settle lower—into hips and drinks and impulse. People used to come to feel something real; now, they came to forget. Vince thrived in it, feeding off the heat and chaos, his lyrics edging further into provocation. Jonas, meanwhile, found himself straining to hear the signal through the noise.

*
**

Backstage one night, while Vince was half-drunk and shouting into a girl's ear over the music, Jonas picked up his guitar and walked outside.

He needed to breathe.

He needed to remember why he started.

He needed to find a way to keep writing songs that meant something — even as the cost of compromise kept rising.

He wandered around the back of the venue, until he found a quiet bench beneath a flickering streetlamp. The night air was cool, the pavement still warm. Jonas sat down with his notebook, opened it to a fresh page, and let the words come. No agenda. No hook. Just a voice trying to find itself again.

That's when it started.

Caught up in a race to find our happiness in things...

He paused, staring at the empty page.

Measuring success in all the dollars that it brings...

The line flickered into being, not as bitterness, but as truth. Hard truth.

The melody was soft at first, almost hesitant. He scribbled

the lines as they came, pausing only to hum a few notes of melody, feeling the shape of it form in his chest. By the time he finished the chorus, he knew. This wasn't just a song. It was a reminder. A vow. A message to his future self:

Don't forget your dreams.

Chapter 13 – The Crossroads Gig

The band was gaining traction. Gigs were coming more frequently now, and not just in dingy dive bars—they were playing clubs with real stages, real sound systems, and increasingly real audiences. The dream was still handmade, but the edges were starting to shine. With that shine, however, came more gear, more travel, and more logistical headaches. Renting trucks for every show was killing their bottom line.

*
**

Jonas's mother, always quietly attuned to the subtle needs in his life, had mentioned something in passing: neighbors of hers in Florida were selling an old panel van. It might be worth checking out, she said. Jonas figured it couldn't hurt. Besides, a solo road trip felt like the right move—he needed room to breathe, and to notice what was changing. Vince was more driven than ever. There was an energy brewing—something restless and sharp.

Florida brought a surprise. The so-called "panel van" turned out to be anything but basic. It was a full custom conversion, clearly someone's pride and joy from a few years back: plush seating, polished aluminum wheels, upholstered ceiling panels, tinted windows, even a subtle mural on the back doors. Jonas laughed when he saw it. This wasn't just a van—it was a statement. He bought it on the spot.

*
**

The drive back north was long, but the van made it feel like a moving meditation. Somewhere in Virginia, he pulled into a small campground to rest. It was dusk, and the trees swayed gently in the golden light. Families were barbecuing, children chased fireflies, and the scent of pine mixed with smoke was in the air. He wasn't expecting anything more than a quiet night.

Then he saw her.

She was younger—clearly not a peer—but there was something magnetic about her presence. She moved through the trees like she belonged to them. Chestnut hair, sun-kissed skin, and a faraway look in her eyes that suggested she was seeing more than what was in front of her. Isabel.

She was on a rare camping trip with her father and sister, she later explained. Her parents had split years ago, and this reunion was some kind of awkward attempt at connection. It wasn't going great. Her sister was sullen, her dad trying too hard. But the woods helped. Music helped more.

Jonas, enchanted, had found some excuse to say hello. He couldn't remember the question—just that she'd answered with a soft smile and then walked away. That night, music played by the communal fire. He had his guitar. She had a love of Jim Croce. Their eyes met across the flickering light. Conversation turned into laughter, then silence. No kiss. Just a spark—honest and alive.

By morning, she was gone.

Until she wasn't. As Jonas merged onto the highway, he caught a flash in his rearview mirror. A car pulled alongside. A window rolled down. Isabel, leaning out, called his name with a grin that lit up the dawn. Then the car sped away. Gone again, but not forgotten.

*
**

Back in New York, Jonas pulled up to the venue with the new van and a strange kind of energy in his chest. Vince was already in gear—lining up shows, finalizing setlists, coordinating with the club's manager. Their next string of gigs included a coveted spot at a showcase that could mean real industry eyes on them.

Their sound had shifted. The sweetness of their early songs had faded into something darker, more aggressive. Songs like

"First Impressions," "Original Sin," "Somewhere Between Heaven and Hell," and "Tell Me Tell Me" filled the setlist. The crowd loved it. Vince fed off the energy, bold and electric on stage. Jonas played his parts, tight and precise, but his thoughts drifted.

To the woods. To the fire. To Isabel's eyes.

*
**

After the show, the buzz lingered. Someone from a known label had been in the audience. Vince was elated. They were close—he could feel it. Jonas smiled, nodded, said all the right things. But later, as he sat alone in the van's velour wrapped silence, he found himself questioning what kind of artist he was becoming.

Isabel had stirred something in him. Not lust. Not infatuation. Awareness. She reminded him that the world didn't need more noise—it needed truth. Even if it came wrapped in crooked smiles and imperfect chords.

The van's engine hummed softly as he turned the key, the road calling once again. Somewhere between heaven and hell, there was a voice he needed to follow. And maybe, if fate allowed, he'd see her again.

Chapter 14 – The Breaking Point

The gigs were going well. Better than well. Jonas and Vince were playing three or four nights a week, bouncing between college towns and small clubs in Connecticut, New York, and New Jersey. Their shows were sharp, their momentum undeniable, and their sets were starting to draw real crowds—not just curious locals but actual fans. It felt like the beginning of something big. But with each show, Jonas could feel something slipping—something harder to name. The crowds were growing, yes. The songs were getting sharper. But the space between him and Vince was stretching thin, like a wire pulled too tight.

*
**

There was one gig that stood out on the calendar: The Bitter End in Greenwich Village—a small venue with a legendary name. The kind of place that carried ghosts in its walls and promises in its stage lights. For Jonas, it was a holy place, an altar to all the singer-songwriters who'd come before. For Vince, it was a launchpad. They'd been told there would be industry people in the room—managers, label scouts, maybe even a known producer or two. Everything was riding on it.

*
**

What Jonas hadn't expected was Isabel.

She showed up at sound-check, like a dream walking back into his life. Eight months and five hundred miles later, and yet it felt like just yesterday. Back in Richmond, on the first night they'd met, Jonas had told stories about the band and what they were trying to do. Isabel had given him her email address, and she'd been quietly keeping track of their schedule through the mailing list the band had set up. She'd even replied to a couple of show updates with short messages —friendly, encouraging, always wishing him luck. But she hadn't let him know she'd be at the Bitter End. That part was a surprise. But seeing her now, standing near the bar with her arms crossed and that half-smile, Jonas felt everything rush back.

*
**

He introduced her to Vince before the show. Vince was his usual charming, loud self—amplified. He flirted shamelessly, making jokes and touching her arm more than once. Jonas had told him about Isabel. Had made it clear how different she was, how important. But Vince either forgot or didn't care. Isabel didn't seem fazed—she handled herself with grace, maybe even amusement. But Jonas saw it for what it was. Disrespect.

*
**

The show was a knockout. The house was full, the crowd loud, and the energy in the room unmistakable. Vince was on fire—more intense, more theatrical, more everything. And the audience loved it. They screamed for encores. A few execs even stood in the back, nodding and whispering.

After the set, the sidewalk outside the venue became a makeshift business meeting. Card exchanges, compliments, offers of drinks. Vince soaked it up like gasoline. He was already talking about "next steps" and "creative flexibility" and "what sells." Jonas stood by Isabel, watching from the edge. He felt hollow. He could already see what came next. The studio sessions, the rewrites, "the compromises." A room full of mirrors, none of them true. If he followed Vince into that world, he knew exactly what he'd lose. Not just the band. Not just Isabel. His voice.

*
**

Later that night, back at the hotel, it came to a head.

"I don't get it," Jonas said. "I know some of the songs are new—that's fine. They're good songs. But what you did tonight... that wasn't about the songs. That was about you.

109

That energy, that attitude—it wasn't what we set out to do. I know we're performing for the crowd—but there used to be something in it that was for *us* too. Tonight, it felt like it was only for them."

"It's what works," Vince shot back. "Yeah, maybe it was more for them tonight—but that's how you break through. Once we're in, we can do whatever we want. Make the kind of music we *really* believe in."

Jonas shook his head slowly. "You keep saying that—but I've been watching you. The closer we get, the further you drift from what we started. You're not coming back to it, Vince. You're already gone."

Vince grabbed a beer from the mini fridge. "You're just over-thinking it. This is how the game's played. Push the energy, push the presence. We got their attention, didn't we?" Jonas stayed quiet for a moment, then looked him dead in the eye. "You crossed a line with Isabel."

Vince scoffed. "She's a grown woman, Jonas. And if she's your girl, maybe you should've made that clear."

Jonas's voice was steady. "It's not about claiming her. It's about the way you acted—like who she is didn't matter. Like she was just another piece of the spotlight. And it's not just her. It's the music. It's the band. You're already treating everything like it's yours to manipulate. You've already sold out, Vince—and we haven't even signed anything yet."

Vince leaned back, arms crossed. "Then don't come with me."

Jonas didn't reply. He didn't need to. Vince's words only confirmed what he already knew. The dream they'd shared wasn't mutual anymore. Maybe it never had been.

The argument didn't end it right then and there. Not officially. But something unspoken had snapped between them.

Jonas packed his guitar, took one last look around the room, and walked out.

*
**

He spent a few nights at the East Village apartment of David Manolis, their occasional piano player. David wasn't surprised when Jonas showed up with his guitar and a duffel bag.

"I figured this was coming," he said. "You want the futon or the floor?"

Over the next few days, Jonas watched the band dissolve in slow motion. Vince stopped calling. Their shared vision evaporated into emails about gear and payment splits.

When the solo offer came, Vince signed without blinking. And Jonas? He didn't fight it. He just... walked away.

After it was all over, Jonas shared an emotional goodbye with David, who clapped a hand on his shoulder and said,

"I'm gonna miss you, man. But keep playing. Just... keep playing."

Jonas nodded, lingering a moment longer than he needed to. Then he climbed into Matilda—the seafoam green, custom conversion van they called Tillie for short. Sleek paint job, tinted windows, polished rims, and a plush interior that had seen long nights, quiet cries, and raucous laughs—it was the kind of cool that didn't need to prove itself. Jonas had fought to keep her in the breakup with Vince, and quietly, he always felt like he'd won. She wasn't just a van; she was memory on wheels, a vessel of freedom, identity, and everything in between.

He had always talked to her like a friend, and today, before turning the key, he thanked her out loud for getting him this far.

He didn't look back when he crossed the bridge out of the city. There was no sadness in the leaving—only the strange, clean ache of something finished. Jonas headed north. He didn't have a plan, just a direction—Connecticut, where Isabel lived. He stopped at a quiet campground off the beaten path near Waterford, paying in cash for a spot by the water. For a while, he lived simply: cooking food over a fire, sleeping under the stars, waking to birdsong instead of sirens.

He called Isabel as soon as he was out of the city, letting

her know he was headed her way. They met up often—walks, late-night talks, shared meals. She didn't push. She just showed up. Steady, clear-eyed, kind.

*
**

One night, after a day spent wandering the shore together and a quiet dinner shared over flickering candles in Tillie's open side door, something shifted. They lingered in a long embrace that turned into something more—tender, reverent, and slow. No need for words. Jonas had never felt anything quite like it. The grief that had lived in the corners of his heart since Paige began to loosen its grip—not disappear, but soften. Isabel didn't try to replace what had been lost. She simply met him where he was and held the space.

Later that night, alone by the fire, Jonas sat with the warmth of her still lingering on his skin. The flames crackled gently as cicadas hummed in the trees and the ocean breeze moved through the leaves in slow waves. He picked up his guitar, not to write, but to feel. His fingers wandered. A melody came. He hummed softly—then paused, as if the words had been waiting for just the right moment. With a quiet breath, he sang the first lines.

Where did I go before I met her?
Who did I know before she came?

Into my heart I've gone and let her
Things will never be the same

Jonas found himself writing again. Not for the crowd. Not for
the charts. For her. For the truth of what had broken and
what remained.

The first new song was called "Isabel."

Part III: The Costs of the Voice

To speak the truth out loud is to risk everything you built on silence.

Chapter 15 – The Open Road

Jonas left just as the trees were finishing their annual blaze of color—late fall, crisp and full of departure. To the outside world, he looked like a drifter: a young man with a guitar, a van, and no fixed address. But in truth, his life was tightly organized behind the scenes—bookings, mileage, gear checks, sleep spots all plotted out in notebooks and memory. He had embraced the bard's path: nomadic, yes, but deliberate.

Performances weren't glamorous—libraries, independent bookstores, coffeehouses on college campuses across the tri-state area—but they were intimate, real. Each show added another thread to the tapestry he was weaving—part witness, part wanderer, part translator of longings people hadn't yet found words for. Isabel's mother and stepfather offered a place to land between gigs—their driveway in Connecticut served as a recurring basecamp. There, he was met with warmth, encouragement, and no questions about stability or five-year plans—only curiosity, good food, and the space to be.

*
**

That winter, Jonas expanded south with the help of a secondhand laptop gifted by Isabel's father. In the evenings, it glowed like a lantern inside Tillie—his map, confirming each stop on a journey charted in lines and miles.

***

By December, his route curved into Florida. He played over 50 shows heading down the coast. In Wakulla Springs, he stopped by to see Elaine and visited his parents in neighboring Crawfordville. Though clearly thriving—healthy, grounded, expressive—he felt a thin veil of disapproval. Polite smiles masked subtle judgment: that this life of parking lots and postcards wasn't a real future. He thought of Isabel's mother, who left warm soup on the stovetop and never asked when he'd get a "real job." The contrast made the humid air there in the Florida panhandle feel even heavier.

***

During a short leg of performances in the West Palm Beach area, Jonas stayed for a few days in Rachel's driveway—just long enough to see his sister between shows, always sleeping in Tillie, his van, as he did everywhere on tour. She was warm at first, until tension surfaced around his use of her address for check payments. She used unfamiliar words like "your associates," and Jonas was caught off guard. He didn't realize it then, but it was the first visible crack in a foundation he'd thought unshakable. Jonas noted how easily Isabel's friends welcomed him into conversations, dinners, even their driveways—no questions asked, no hidden signals or subtle terms to decode. Rachel's words hinted at something deeper— boundaries cloaked in careful language, leaving Jonas to decode the meaning on his own.

*
**

By spring, his itinerary carried him north again—Georgia to South Carolina, through North Carolina, and back into Virginia. Each stop had been booked months in advance, the path not spontaneous but deliberately carved. In one small town, Isabel's grandparents showed up for a bookstore show and, afterward, invited him home for dinner—a warm meal served with stories and second helpings. They became recurring hosts on future loops, offering food, warmth, and easy conversation. There was no need to prove anything to them. No performance of responsibility, no mask of ambition. Just the pleasure of presence. A quiet affirmation that family wasn't always about shared history or names on a mailbox— it was about who made space for you without conditions. And sometimes, that wasn't the family you were born into.

Compared to the din of bars, these sober, attentive gatherings helped Jonas articulate something he had only intuited before: "My job is to observe, reflect, and—if I'm lucky—offer something back that makes people feel seen."

*
**

It was in North Carolina that Isabel made the decision to join the journey—not just from afar as she had for months, but in person, fully. They'd talked about it for weeks—casual mentions that became real questions, and eventually, a plan. When she stepped into the van with her duffel and her smile, something shifted. Her presence grounded the road.

While Isabel scrolled through a message board looking for coffeehouse gigs, she nudged Jonas with a half-smile. "Your old band's making noise again," she said. Vince had posted show dates in major cities, photos in dark sunglasses, all swagger and smoke. Jonas raised an eyebrow, but said nothing. There was something familiar in it—and something he no longer missed.

That night, they sat around a small fire ringed with stones, the air soft with pine smoke and laughter. Isabel introduced Jonas to a simple dice game she used to play, now re-imagined in a cast-iron frying pan. The clatter of dice on metal echoed through the campground in a way that always drew attention. Campers strolled over, curious smiles on their faces, often saying the same thing: they didn't know why, but they knew it was a game—and they wanted in.

Isabel's grandmother, who worked in bulk mail, occasionally sent boxes of uncanceled stamps— tokens of thrift, a quiet rebellion. Around their picnic-table "studio," those stamps found new life. Dice games drew kids in; postcards and glue sticks drew the adults. In this unlikely roadside rhythm, art and connection blurred. Isabel kept their growing network alive with handwritten notes and handcrafted charm. It wasn't just outreach—it was how they built a life. And somehow, amid the laughter, the glue sticks, and the dice, they even gained new fans.

Of course, the dream had a practical side. They learned to source ice, find clean water, and camp stealthily. They marked the best camping spots, spigots, and $1 theaters in a physical atlas. One day, they were skinny dipping below a waterfall when a tour bus of Chinese tourists arrived. There was laughter, scrambling, and a memory etched in both embarrassment and joy.

This wasn't escapism—it was experiment. A question: could you live simply, stay creative, and make a living outside the system? The costly hotel, motel, and restaurant experiences of his days with Vince and the band had long since been traded for van nights in Tillie, hammocks strung between trees, and healthy meals with fresh ingredients cooked over an open fire. Mornings arrived with birdsong, not check-out deadlines. In contrast to the Echo's polished illusions, this was life at its most textured and alive.

*
**

At a serene lake deep in Georgia, they found what felt like a sacred place. Quiet, untouched, timeless. They stayed for days. The stillness gave his songs room to unfold—Wounded Trees, Where Did We Come From, Happy Man—each one a quiet reckoning with freedom, loss, and the search for meaning.

Yet, beneath the songs and postcards, an unease had started to stir. Why the subtle chill from family? What had changed? He didn't know why the people who should have known him best felt suddenly distant—while near-strangers offered kinship without condition. The questions floated quietly, unanswered, like static beneath a beautiful melody. One line from a new song came to mind—*Where did we come from... how'd we get here...* He hadn't yet connected the meaning, but the past was starting to hum, and its signal was getting stronger.

*
**

Still, the road held them. And for now, Jonas was at peace with the rhythm of the unknown. He had food, purpose, and someone beside him who understood. Gratitude hummed beneath it all—even as the first hints of dissonance began to emerge.

Chapter 16 – Fuel, Fire, and Family

The Everglades had been paradise—until it wasn't. Jonas and Isabel had lost track of time among the swampy stillness, reading aloud from the stack of books they'd gathered on their journey, cooking over the fire, skinny-dipping with the alligators. Rangers had reassured them the gators were more afraid of them than they were of the gators. They also taught them a trick—if an alligator kept the same distance no matter how you moved, it hadn't been fed by humans and still filed you under too big, too much trouble—not lunch. That trick worked like a charm allowing them to enjoy the waters of the Everglades while they were there. They had let go of their wilderness fears—at least when it came to alligators.

That night by the fire, the gator trick still fresh in their minds, Jonas pulled out his notebook. He'd been toying with a song called *Where Did We Come From* for weeks, but something had been missing. As the fire cracked and Isabel rolled a cigarette in the orange glow, he scratched out new lines: *"Take a walk back / Half a million years / A world full of balance / Not wilderness fears."* The irony wasn't lost on him—

how understanding the balance of nature could calm a primal fear, while the balance of their own bank account quietly slipped out of sync. But the song was too alive to stop now, and he gave in to the muse, not the math.

*
**

By the time they got back on the road, they were down to their last hundred dollars. One hundred miles and nearly a week still separated them from their next scheduled performance. It was the first time Jonas truly felt the edge of their chosen lifestyle—that sharp reality of living outside the Echo's carefully netted economy. Panic hit fast and hard. He pulled the van over and got out to walk, his breath shallow, thoughts racing. For all their ideals and creative fire, they'd miscalculated. The van got just ten miles to the gallon, provisions weren't free, and they had six days and a hundred miles to go on a hundred dollars. This wasn't about scarcity or shame—it was simple math, and they were cutting it close.

Isabel watched Jonas pacing for a few minutes, then got out of the van and joined him on his walk. She took his hand and they sat down together in the grass just off the roadside, the hum of distant traffic blending with the sound of wind in the trees. There, she reminded him gently of how far they'd come, of the hundreds of people they'd reached, the shows ahead, the crafts she'd been selling, the merch that still moved. She wasn't wrong. Within two weeks, they would be back on their feet—flea markets, busking, a couple of decent merchandise sales, even a booking from someone who'd seen Jonas play in a bookstore months before. The Echo may chart the maps and run the marketplace, but there was still space to breathe outside its borders.

*
**

They spent a week at Jonas's parents' house. It was meant to be a reset—help with repainting, do some laundry, eat a few meals. For Jonas, it was also a quiet test—an unspoken invitation to begin again. Part of him still hoped for repair between him and his father, even if no one dared to name the damage. Isabel rolled up her sleeves and grabbed a brush, but her first real encounter with Jonas's father didn't go well. He barked at her for not cutting in the edges cleanly. She didn't argue, she just put down the brush and walked away. That was Isabel. But Jonas had to call him on it. It didn't escalate, but it didn't vanish either. The older Jonas got, the harder it became to excuse the man's tone.

That moment, as small as it seemed, was enough. Jonas had held onto a quiet hope that something might shift, that the two of them could one day name what had passed between them and move forward. But when even kindness from Isabel met with criticism, he knew: there would be no naming. No repair. Just more meanness—dressed in habit, not love.

Still, they didn't linger. By the next morning, they were already discussing routes and gas prices.

*
**

The stop at his sister Elaine's place was shorter. She had a new partner—funny, a little goofy, and clearly eager to make a strong impression. Jonas liked him at first; his charm was disarming, his energy upbeat. But underneath the jokes and easy banter, something felt off. Back when Jonas first started playing in bars after high school, Elaine had looked up to him —he was her hero in more ways than he ever realized. Over the years, especially through her tough breakups, he'd been the one she called to help pick up the pieces.

Now, things had shifted. Her new partner seemed to know Jonas had once occupied that pedestal. Maybe that explained the way he overplayed his presence—cracking jokes a little too loudly, inserting himself into every conversation. Jonas didn't take it personally, but he couldn't help but feel the temperature change. Elaine seemed happy, and that mattered most. Jonas began to sense something quietly shifting: the way Elaine saw him wasn't quite the same. Where she'd once looked up to him, her view now seemed filtered through her partner's impressions—and perhaps through her own discomfort with the choices he had made. It wasn't just her perception that shifted, but the version of him she now shared with others too. And maybe that version... was beginning to drift from the truth.

*
**

And then came the judgments—the ones that never arrived in conversation but landed later, in letters. Elaine, whose humor was rarely just humor, told Jonas she thought he looked like a drug addict. She meant it. He laughed it off, but Isabel saw the sting. Isabel noticed that Jonas was lean, yes—but it came from hiking, camping, and clean food. Jonas, meanwhile, couldn't help but notice how leanness was praised in someone with a gym membership and a steady job, but in someone like him—on the road, living differently—it suddenly looked like decay. And then there was Isabel's hand-rolled cigarettes, which Jonas secretly loved the ritual of—watching her under the stars by the fire, hands deliberate, lips soft—which also seemed to draw quiet scorn.

In another letter much later, Elaine would admit that the "drug addict" comment wasn't hers—it came from her partner, but she'd repeated it. That same letter mentioned concern that Jonas was smoking—claimed he'd said it was to manage stress. It didn't ring true, but something about it tugged at a memory. He thought back to a moment on the back porch, a quiet evening when Elaine had joined Isabel outside. Isabel had just rolled a cigarette, relaxed, open, maybe explaining having been asked, "I enjoy it. And sure, it helps if I'm stressed." Jonas remembered joining them for a moment and taking a few drags himself—he loved the ritual of it, not the habit. But now, piecing things together, it felt like fragments of that evening had been gathered and rearranged into a new story—one that better matched the worries and judgments taking shape. Not long after, Rachel chimed in from another direction, writing a letter that implied he was homeless, a drifter, that he "imparted darkness" when he visited. That he came only because he had nowhere else to go. They hadn't said any of it to his face. But it was becoming clear—they'd been saying it to each other. And it was unsettling.

*
**

That night, parked beneath a canopy of trees, Isabel stayed quiet at first. Then she reached for Jonas's hand.

"You know who you are," she said. "So do I."

It wasn't advice. It wasn't reassurance. Just truth. And it

helped.

*
**

They drove on in silence for a while, letting the trees and passing towns do the talking. On the road, Jonas and Isabel had always noticed the differences from state to state—how some towns embraced them like wandering sages, offering meals, venues, and kindness. Others greeted them with suspicion, eyes narrowing at the van, the guitars, Isabel's handmade jewelry. Sometimes strangers leaned in—curious, open, asking questions. Sometimes they cried, touched by a lyric, a moment, a truth that felt familiar

*
**

But those were the strangers.

Back home, the people who were supposed to know him best—his own family—saw something else entirely. While some strangers glimpsed freedom and light in his life, his family seemed to spot only shadows. The contrast was confusing. How could those furthest from him see something hopeful, while those closest to him saw only risk? Or recklessness? That question lingered like smoke in the van.

*
**

A few nights later, camped by a quiet lake between gigs, they sat side by side by the fire, hands wrapped around tin mugs, boots near the coals.

Jonas stared into the flames, then turned to Isabel.

"Do you ever look back and wonder if we turned so hard toward freedom, we missed a sign saying we weren't supposed to?"

She smiled, sipping from her mug.

"Yeah... like maybe there was a sign—tucked behind an old tree, half-faded, in a language we don't speak."

He laughed.

"Right? Something carved into a log in Old Norse—'turn back, ye dreamers.'"

Isabel laughed and leaned in, poking at the fire with a stick.

"Or maybe it said, 'This way is steep, unpredictable, and filled with moments that will make you question everything. Proceed if you dare.'"

Jonas raised his mug in mock salute.

"Guess we dared."

She clinked his cup.

"And here we are."

He looked down at his notebook, flipping through a few dog-eared pages, then said softly,

"Maybe it's not about the 'right' way or the 'wrong' one."

She nodded, eyes reflecting the firelight.

"Yeah. Maybe it's about the path you've chosen—and the compass you trust to keep you on it. Even when the world tells you to turn around."

He wrote that line down.

The flames danced between them, the night quiet enough to hear a single owl from the trees above. Somewhere between the pages, the melody began to take shape—not as a song of certainty, but of searching. It asked the question the Echo never did: Which way is the right way... and how would I know?

*
**

"The Right Way" didn't arrive in frustration or doubt—it came quietly, like a companion to their questions by the fire. It wasn't a lament. It was a mirror. One that reflected a culture afraid to move, to choose, to trust. Jonas had seen it before—in others, and in himself. The song wondered aloud whether right and wrong were even useful questions anymore... or just more noise from the Echo. It asked something simpler instead: What if you can't trust the compass until you've questioned who set its north?

Which way is the right way,

When I'm standing at a fork in the road.
Which way is the wrong way,
Is this the road to ruin,
I wonder, how would I know.
Which way is the right way,

*
**

The highs stretched them. The lows tested them. But through it all, they found their center—not by escaping the Echo, but by returning, again and again, to the Voice.

Chapter 17 – The Loss of Izzy

They called it a pilgrimage of thought and wonder.

Bookstores became sanctuaries. While Jonas strummed songs between poetry shelves and philosophy corners, Isabel hunted the stacks like a scholar with a sixth sense. She was the curator of their shared journey—seeking out titles that cracked open questions, not just answered them. Walden, Ishmael, The Soul's Code, Silent Spring—these weren't just books; they were trail markers on a road less traveled.

Jonas would finish a set and find Isabel cross-legged in the aisle, completely absorbed, a pile of chosen titles beside her. Sometimes they read aloud to each other by firelight, sometimes in silence, side by side, each unraveling a thread of understanding. These were their richest days—sun-drenched afternoons in hammocks woven into the stillness between gigs, late-night talks under stars, their bond pulsing with the rhythm of shared discovery and unspoken dreams.

Jonas had been writing all along, but during this season the songs shifted. They felt quieter, clearer—less driven, more essential. One song in particular, *The Good Life*, became a kind of anthem for their wandering values. Inspired by the books Isabel brought into their orbit and the slow beauty of their days, it carried the ache of another possible world.

Give me a good life
One fueled by passion
For earth and nurture
Not cash and fashion…

The songs were intended to name the unnamed, to connect what the world kept apart. They were reflections—soundtracks to their wandering, to the freedom they were living. A few lines borrowed from Rachel Carson, a melody shaped by a sunset, a chorus inspired by something Isabel said in passing. She was often his spark, though she never claimed that role.

Their creative rhythm was so alive, Jonas barely noticed the first rumblings of trouble in the distance.

*
**

It came in the form of a phone call from David Manolis, their occasional piano player from the early days. David had always been more observer than participant, but his ear was everywhere.

"Thought you might want to know," he said. "Vince's deal fell apart. Only managed to get four tracks on an EP before things blew up."

Jonas stayed quiet. David went on.

"Word is he was pushing too hard, acting out. Burned the band, scared the label. Nobody wants to touch it now. He's back in town, bouncing around. Looks rough."

Jonas didn't gloat. He closed his eyes, searching for the shape of what he felt but couldn't name. There was a strange emptiness in hearing the news. A space Vince once occupied—competitor, friend, antagonist—was now quiet.

But Jonas had no time to dwell. The road called, and Isabel was still beside him.

For now.

*
**

It came one morning, quietly—just a missed call and a voicemail with no details. Isabel's face changed the moment she heard it. She didn't explain, not fully. She just said it was something from before. Before Jonas. Before the road.

They drove north without discussing much. Her silence was full of meaning—tight, not angry. Jonas didn't press. He could feel the weight she carried, and whatever it was, she wasn't ready to share it. Not yet.

It wasn't until a diner stop on the Connecticut border that she finally spoke.

"I did something stupid a couple years ago," she said over

black coffee gone cold. "It was small. But not harmless. A protest that got out of hand. Some damage... and a security camera. I thought it was behind me. But I guess the case got reopened."

Jonas nodded slowly. Not out of judgment, but out of trying to understand. "Are you in danger?"

She shook her head. "Not exactly. But I need to turn myself in before they come looking. I won't put you in that kind of spotlight. I won't let them use you to find me."

The silence that followed wasn't empty. It was full of grief —unspoken, but mutual.

Jonas drove her the rest of the way to her hometown. No music, no words, just the steady hum of the highway. When they reached the town's edge, Isabel finally reached over and touched his hand.

"I'm scared, Jonas. Not of jail, exactly. Just... of losing this. The air. The road. The quiet. You."

Jonas looked over, his voice low but sure. "I promise you... what we've had out here—the quiet, the good life—it can't be erased. You can't be erased, Izzy. I'll wait, if you want me to."

"You helped me live a better version of myself," she said.

His hand tightened on the steering wheel, fighting the ache that rose in his throat. He wanted to tell her she'd done the same for him. But the words didn't come.

She stepped out of the van with her backpack and a weathered case packed with colored pencils, a tattered sketchpad, and a few boxes of beads. She didn't look back.

Jonas waited until she disappeared through the doors of the police station. Then he pulled away, slowly, into a road that suddenly felt far too quiet.

*
**

That first night without her was all edges. The van—Tillie—once a moving haven, now echoed. Even she felt different—quiet in a way that made Jonas ache. Her absence wasn't just emotional; it It changed how everything sat inside it. The passenger seat looked startled by its own vacancy.

He parked near a coastal town Isabel had always wanted to visit but never did. Slept with one eye open. Woke up with the kind of loneliness that doesn't announce itself, just settles in like fog. Long ago, he'd wondered if losing someone whose heart beat close to his own would bring a different kind of loneliness.

Now he knew it would. And did.

At a grocery store lot outside of town, it caught him off guard. A man pulled up beside the van while Jonas was shifting gear in the back. The man's son, maybe twelve, pointed and laughed.

"Look at the freak show," the boy shouted, loud enough for anyone nearby to hear.

Jonas didn't flinch. He was used to the glances, the suspicion. But something about this one stuck. Maybe it was the boy's eyes, mirroring the man's disdain. Maybe it was the part of Jonas that still half-expected the father to step in, to offer some correction. Instead, the man said nothing—just stared, his silence an approval.

Maybe it was the sudden realization that no one was there to buffer it.

Before, Isabel might've cracked a joke, disarmed the moment, softened the sharp edge of being seen as a threat. Now, Jonas just closed the van slowly and drove away. Not because he was afraid. But because he was beginning to understand something hard to name—that once someone's convinced themselves of who you are, even your silence gets cast in their play.

And if you try to speak, you're only reciting their lines.

*
**

He kept driving.

The next couple of months settled into a kind of rhythm. Jonas kept to his schedule—bookstore sets, college shows, coffeehouse gigs that paid predictably and kept the wheels turning. The routine helped. It gave shape to the days, even if something essential felt missing.

Without Isabel, the quiet changed shape. It didn't invite reflection anymore—it just bounced his own thoughts back at him, louder and lonelier. Her absence softened some joys, dulled some songs. But inspiration still found him: in conversations after shows, in the questions students asked, in the eyes of someone who truly listened.

He filled notebooks and made voice memos wherever the road left room—campgrounds when he could, city corners when he had to. In nature, the songs felt like companions. In the city, they came with side glances and second thoughts. But still, he wrote. Sometimes, in rare moments, he caught glimpses of what he and Isabel had shared—a spark of understanding between strangers, a shared reverence for something unspoken.

*
**

Then came Florida.

He'd driven down the East Coast, aiming to reach a show scheduled for that evening. With a few hours to spare, he pulled into a legal beach-side parking spot—public space, money in the meter, guitar over his shoulder. It was the kind of afternoon he'd learned to treasure: sun-warmed skin, salt in the air, sand still on his feet.

A man in his sixties emerged from a restaurant nearby, red-faced and insistent. He claimed the space Jonas had parked in was "for customers only," despite no signage to support the claim. Jonas, trying to deescalate, simply walked back toward the meter to add time.

The man followed, shouting. And then—an attack. Jonas, caught off guard, had his back turned. All his energy went into shielding the guitar strapped to his shoulder.

Police arrived within minutes. The restaurant owner had already pulled his employees into a huddle. Their story was aligned.

An officer approached Jonas and asked him to step aside. Another took his guitar. Without further questions, they turned him around and cuffed his wrists. Metal bit into skin. His feet were bare.

One of the café witnesses started to object, voice raised, but was hushed by a friend.

The restaurant staff stood in a cluster, arms crossed, watching. One of them smirked.

A patrol car door opened. Jonas ducked his head and slid in, the cuffs still tight behind his back.

A few yards away, three college-aged diners stood frozen

beside their half-eaten lunch. One of them—a lanky kid with a guitar pick looped around his wrist—stepped forward. "That's not what happened," he said. His voice cracked, but he didn't stop. "He didn't do anything. That guy attacked him."

Another added, "We watched the whole thing. He never touched the guy. Just tried to walk away."

Their friend, who'd been filming casually for fun with a small hand-held video camera—he was into that kind of thing—flipped it open and rewound the tape. "We've got it. It's all here."

The officers paused. One walked over, took the camera, and began reviewing the footage. A second officer pulled out a notepad, asked for names. The group gave them, fast and clear.

Back near the restaurant, the owner and his staff fell quiet.

Jonas sat in the back of the car, staring out the side window, unaware of what was unfolding. He wouldn't know until later how close he'd come to being erased by someone else's story—and how a handful of strangers had chosen, in that moment, to tell the truth.

A few minutes later, the officer returned and opened the door. "You're free to go," he said, voice steady but softer now. "Those young folks at the café saw what happened. One of them caught it on video. You're lucky they spoke up."

Jonas stepped out, wrists still marked from the cuffs.

The officer handed back his guitar, then hesitated. "We'll be following up with the restaurant. There are consequences for false reports." He paused again. "Sorry you were put through that."

Jonas took the guitar, the weight of it oddly reassuring in his hands. He opened his mouth to speak, but nothing came. He gave a small nod, more reflex than response.

The students were still nearby, standing awkwardly beside their table. Jonas crossed the sidewalk toward them.

"You saved me," he said simply.

The one with the video camera gave a nervous smile. "Nah, we just... couldn't not say something."

Jonas looked at each of them. "You didn't just say something. You saw. And you chose to speak."

There was a beat of silence.

The kid with the guitar pick blurted, "Where are you headed next?"

Jonas smiled, a little crooked. "Up the coast. Some gigs lined up, some I'll find on the way. Still chasing songs. Still figuring it out."

They exchanged names. A napkin became an address

book. Jonas promised to send music; they promised to come find him if he ever passed through their campus town.

It wasn't a full restoration. But it was something. A reminder that not everyone slept through the Echo's lies. That truth could still rise, sometimes, when someone had the courage to *witness*.

*
**

That's when it became clear: even with witnesses, even with restraint, a life outside the Echo came with its own risks. You didn't have to do anything wrong. You just had to be somewhere you weren't expected.

It was the third time now.

First, a couple outside a venue—tense glances, shifting postures, fear without provocation.

Then, the boy and his father—verbal disgust passed down like an heirloom.

And now, this: a physical confrontation, a rewritten story—almost believed—and an identity nearly rewritten by force.

Jonas sat with it—not the pain, not the fear, but the pattern.

He'd stepped outside the story the Echo told. And the Echo responded, not with curiosity, but with correction. It wasn't personal. That was the most chilling part. It was systemic. Reflexive.

There was nothing left to explain. But everything left to understand.

*
**

He stopped at places he and Isabel had loved—bookstores where she'd curled up on the floor, cafés where they shared quiet mornings over coffee, college towns where they'd felt like conspirators in something quietly revolutionary. But now, those places felt like exhibits in a museum: present, but behind glass. Her laughter no longer echoed. Her questions no longer lingered. He hadn't just lost her. He'd lost the version of the world that came with her.

At a campus show in North Carolina, he played *The Good Life* to a packed room. Students swayed, sang along, linked arms on the chorus like it was a movement. For a moment, he let himself watch them—beautiful, full of belief. But something in him stayed quiet.

They didn't know the person who made that song matter.

It wasn't just Isabel. It was what lived between them. The current. The resonance. The way relationship could amplify even the smallest joy, magnify beauty into meaning.

The Good Life hadn't come from solitude. It had come from connection.

He wasn't ready to say all of that out loud. But the

knowing had begun. Like a note still vibrating in the air long after the last chord had faded.

*
**

That night, he called Thomas. It had been weeks since they'd spoken, and the moment Jonas heard his voice, something inside him softened.

They talked about everything and nothing—the road, the food, the weather in Charlotte. Jonas didn't mention Isabel directly, but Thomas knew. He always did.

Near the end of the call, Thomas said quietly, "You're still out there for a reason. Just keep going. Write it down. Play it out. Let it say what you can't."

Jonas hung up and stared out the windshield for a long time. Then he pulled out his notebook and wrote the first lines of a new song. Not out of inspiration exactly—but necessity.

Around the fire that night, the words came into shape:

Keep on keeping on
Never give up the fight...
Keep on keeping on
Everything will be all right...

It wasn't a declaration. It was a reminder. A hand on his own shoulder. A rhythm to walk by. The song wasn't about winning. It was about moving. One breath, one verse, one mile at a time.

*
**

Weeks passed. The shows continued. He sold some merch, restocked the van, made a few new connections. But something in him stayed elsewhere—hovering behind the rhythm of his routine.

He was back in Virginia when he first heard. A voice-mail came through from Lena Calder, one of the student organizers at Glenford College. Jonas had played there a handful of times over the years. They remembered him and Isabel as a team—part music, part philosophy, part something else entirely.

"Hey Jonas," Lena's voice said, a little hesitant. "I just wanted to say thanks again for your last set. People here still talk about it. And… I'm not sure if I should even say this, but I saw Isabel at a show last night. She was with someone—a guy, I think his name was Vince? I guess I just assumed you two were still out there together. Anyway, it caught me off guard. Thought you'd want to know."

Jonas didn't move. He didn't even hang up the phone for a while after the message ended. He just sat there, staring at the wall of the van for a long time.

He told himself it wasn't betrayal. She'd made her choice. She was free.

But the feeling that followed had nothing to do with logic.

*
**

The next day, he found himself heading toward the town where he knew Isabel had stayed. He told himself it was just on the way—that he'd keep driving. But something tugged at him.

He knew where her trailer would be. She'd mentioned the spot more than once—a quiet pull-through behind the community center where the sun hit just right in the mornings.

He told himself it was a bad idea, that no good would come from stopping. But the van slowed anyway. Before he could second-guess himself further, he was already pulling into the gravel lot.

There it was. Unmistakable.

He knocked. The door opened.

Vince.

He looked like someone trying not to look like someone who had something to hide—nervous smile, hands in pockets, too much casual energy.

"Hey man," Vince said. "Wasn't expecting—uh, how's the road?"

Jonas didn't answer right away. He just looked past Vince, into the dim space behind him. Then back at Vince.

"What is this?" he asked, quiet and even.

Vince's mouth opened, then closed. "It's not—it's just... we're talking. Catching up. You know how things go."

Jonas shook his head, not in anger, but because it was so predictably Vince. A man always armed with the most inadequate version of the truth.

He turned to leave.

"Jonas—" Isabel's voice called from inside. He was already halfway to the van when he heard her voice. She stepped out after him, barefoot on the gravel.

"I'm sorry," she said. Soft. Unscripted.

He paused, his back still turned.

In the driver's side window, he could just make out her reflection—barefoot, standing in the gravel, arms folded across her chest. A sting rose behind his eyes, sudden and hot. For a moment, his body leaned toward turning, but he didn't. Instead, he opened the door, climbed in, and started the engine.

Then he pulled away—slowly, quietly—leaving behind everything he didn't know how to hold.

*
**

That night, Jonas didn't grieve the end of a relationship. He grieved something rarer—the slow unraveling of a bond not just of love, but of listening. There had once been a shared current between them, a quiet alignment that held even at a distance. He used to feel the Voice alive in their connection.

But now, the Voice—once between them—had gone still.

Chapter 18 – Defining Moments

It was a Tuesday night in a tiny South Carolina town, the kind of place where everything closed early except the bar that doubled as a café on weekends. Jonas had been booked to play for a dozen people, maybe fewer. He didn't care about the number. Whether it was one person or a thousand, Jonas gave everything he had. Every note, every word—even the silences between them—was an offering.

He'd chosen places like this on purpose—warm, welcoming spaces that didn't need his music to be delightful, but made room for it when it arrived. That made it easier to let go, to play with abandon, to trust the song would land where it needed to.

*
**

The room was humble—dim lighting, folding chairs, a single mic stand on a rug that didn't quite cover the scuffed wood floor. Among the handful of attendees was a man in his late forties or early fifties, sitting with his wife and two teenage girls. They looked like they belonged there—comfortably familiar with the space and each other, open but quiet. But when Jonas played "Leave It All Behind," the man didn't just listen. He heard it.

During "A Good Life," the man leaned forward, his elbows on his knees, eyes fixed on Jonas as if he were decoding something unspoken. By the time Jonas reached the end of "I'm Just Looking," there was a stillness in the air—something unsaid, but deeply felt.

After the show, the man sent his family home. Jonas was packing up cables when the man walked over, hesitated, then said, "I don't know what's happening to me, but I think I've been asleep most of my life."

Jonas didn't respond right away. He just nodded, slowly, giving the man room.

"I didn't choose this life," the man continued. "Not really. It just... happened. Job. Mortgage. Routine. Now I wake up every day and feel like I'm watching someone else live it."

He didn't have all the words—but Jonas knew. That flicker in his eyes—the first crack in the wall. The man didn't know it yet, but he was beginning to see the Echo.

*
**

They kept talking. For nearly two hours. The man asked questions, not about the music, but about why Jonas had written those songs. About what it meant to leave things behind. About whether it was too late to start listening to a Voice he could barely hear.

They stayed in touch. Emails, phone calls. Jonas didn't call himself a mentor. But quietly, he thought of it as something more—a Voice sponsor.

*
**

Months later, the man sent Jonas a letter—handwritten. In it, he described his first act of resistance. Nothing dramatic. Just a single decision: turning down a promotion that would have paid more but demanded even more of his life. It wasn't just a job decision. It was a declaration. And more than that, a transformation.

The letter was humble in tone but seismic in spirit. The man had begun living differently. He'd stopped running from his fears and started moving toward his heart's desires. He'd reclaimed time with his family, spoke more honestly with his wife, and told his daughters things he once thought he'd take to the grave.

The transformation wasn't loud, but it was real—and lasting.

*
**

Jonas couldn't help but think back to another moment—one steeped in silence, but of a different kind. In the fall a year or so back, he'd been parked outside a popular bookstore café where he regularly performed. Guitar in the back, long hair tied back, dressed as he always was—casual, clean, unmistakably himself. The couple who exited the café that evening—well-dressed, polished—saw only a threat. The man kept watch while his wife climbed into their Lexus. They locked the doors without a word. The woman's disapproving glance lingered like a verdict. She didn't need to say a word— the Echo spoke through her eyes. Moments later, Jonas walked into the venue—and the room erupted in cheers and applause.

He had learned this lesson before: the world sees what it wants to see. Angel or threat. Genius or deviant. All within the span of a few breaths.

That quiet revolution in a single life became the seed for a new song: "I'm Not Free at All."

The contrast between that man's transformation and the memory of a darker moment wasn't lost on Jonas. He thought of that day in the parking lot, how a glance could brand him a threat, how silence could feel like judgment. But this was different. The man's letter reminded him that even in a world of misunderstanding, connection was still possible. Influence could still ripple outward.

Inspired, Jonas picked up his guitar and began scribbling

lyrics on a legal pad. The first verse came quickly:

Once upon a time, when the road was home,
I met a man who saw something he'd never known—
Hidden in a song I'd played not long before.
He said, "I heard it, and my jaw dropped to the floor.
How could I have missed what's now so crystal clear—
In a minor-chorded moment, caffeinated concert hall."

It came out of him fast. Raw. Honest. Not about the man, exactly—but about the moment he had seen unfold. A moment that reaffirmed everything Jonas had risked by walking this path. The isolation, the doubt, the scraping by. It all felt worth it.

Not because the world was listening. But because one person had.

As his last chord faded into the night, Jonas felt something he couldn't ignore—an ache not for applause, but for sustainability. For a way to share this resonance without burning himself out in the process.

If one person could wake up... what if the message could reach them without him always being the one to deliver it?

He didn't know the answer yet. But he could feel the question rising.

And that, too, was a kind of clarity.

*
**

He woke early the next morning, the clarity still with him—calm, not electric. He packed the van without fanfare and turned north. There were still eight weeks left on the calendar, shows already booked. He'd play them. But something had shifted.

He stopped accepting new dates.

Town by town, he honored the commitments already made—small clubs, cafés, songwriter circles. But now, with each set, he played like an observer as much as a performer. He shifted the order of songs, changed transitions, watched the room not for applause but for *something else*. For posture shifts. For stillness. For faces caught in thought or caught in tears. Visual resonance.

He began to see it—how the order shaped the experience. How one song, well placed, could open a crack. Another, placed just right, could send something tumbling through. Not just impact. Sequence. Code.

At each stop, he offered quiet goodbyes. Let longtime fans and familiar venues know that this would likely be his last pass through town for a while. No big announcement—just a promise: a special album was coming. He asked them to stay in touch.

The road home took him through six states and a thousand memories. Somewhere along the winding edge of Virginia, in a stretch of trees he knew by heart, her face flashed in his mind—Isabel. The girl in the trees. The first time he saw her, she'd looked back at him like she already knew.

By the 1st of August he reached the gentle hills of Western Massachusetts, the precise order of the album had taken shape in his notebook, and a new urgency was taking root. He didn't head straight for the city, but to a small township just beyond the creative hum of Northampton—close enough to find collaborators, quiet enough to hear himself think. The kind of place where stone walls lined the back roads, where coffee shops doubled as open mics, and strangers talked like they'd known you for years.

He found a modest place to settle, surrounded by trees that felt like they were listening.

That evening, he sent a message to the band:

"I've been working on something I think matters. I'd like to come down and share it with you guys, if you're open."

Chapter 19 – The Live Album and Transition

The responses came quickly. No hesitation. Simon, Calder, and David were all in. They set a date three weeks out—August 28th.

Jonas spent those weeks getting his place in order, settling into a rhythm that felt like forward motion. One afternoon, he found the notebook again—the small one he'd once tucked in the back of a drawer, a place for thoughts he wasn't ready to share. Folded between the pages was the coffeehouse napkin. The ink had bled in one corner, but the four lines were still there. He read them slowly, then picked up a pen. Not to revise, just to finish. The words that came weren't polished or clever, but they felt like a home he'd never stopped building. It wasn't about returning to what was—it was about honoring what had stayed.

Jonas smiled softly as he completed the poem he'd started so many years ago in the coffeehouse. He knew in that moment that "Tulips Don't Wait" belonged on the album. And so he returned to the task of arranging his space with quiet precision—the practiced instinct of someone who'd lived in motion long enough to know how little was truly needed. A chair by the window. A clean table for notebooks. A guitar stand, not far from the woodstove. Everything served the work. Nothing dulled the signal. After years in a van arranged like a spacecraft—tight, essential, focused—he knew how to create an environment that let the mind move freely.

Then, in the hush of one slow afternoon, a letter surfaced—his father's handwriting.

He read it slowly, without reaction. Just observation. Clipped, dismissive. Intellectualized rejection dressed in civility. No interest in dialogue. No space for reflection. Just judgment.

Jonas didn't recoil. He breathed.

He had long since stopped looking for family in those unwilling to see him clearly. The family he built now was one of shared values, mutual recognition, and chosen love. Still, he had tried—consulting professional mediators, extending one last hand through carefully chosen words. No one responded with openness. Not with curiosity. Just silence or scorn.

And that, in its own way, was an answer.

He folded the letter with care. No anger. No grief. Just the closing of a file he'd kept longer than he should. He thought of the rare laugh at the dinner table, the quiet ride to the animal shelter, the compliment passed like a secret between strangers. Hints that maybe, someday, things might shift. But the letter made one thing clear: the file could be closed.

So he returned to his process. With clarity. With peace.

*
**

The time flew by. On the 27th, Jonas packed a few things in the van and headed south toward New York. They met up in a quiet spot outside the city, just the four of them. Jonas told them the story, short and direct. What happened in South Carolina. The shift. The clarity. How he finally knew the order the songs were meant to be in and why.

He didn't ask for much—just a few days, a couple of rehearsals, one studio, and their trust.

After the first run-through, something had shifted in the room. It wasn't just tight—it was alive. Calder caught their eyes, a grin already forming. "Hey," he said. "What if we played a set before we record? I can get us into The Quarry midweek—invite our favorite people. Could be fun."

Everyone nodded. No one needed convincing.

Simon said it first. "Let's do it."

The night they played The Quarry felt like something old being made new again. For Jonas, it wasn't just another gig—

it was a ritual. A crossing.

The room had history. So did the players. Calder on drums. Simon on bass. David on piano. The original lineup—minus Vince. Not as a statement, but as a truth. What remained was what mattered.

That night in that room—what they played, what they felt—it was enough. Not to go back, but to move something forward.

Calder cleared time in his studio's schedule, no questions asked. He mic'd the room like a craftsman, taking care to capture what made it breathe. David came in from his apartment in the East Village, having barely touched a piano in months, and still—when his hands landed, it was like no time had passed. Simon showed up early, unpacked slowly, nodded once. Ready.

No overdubs. No retakes. Just the sound of four people listening—to each other, to the room, to something larger than themselves. It wasn't perfect, but that's what made it true. Jonas didn't need to explain that anymore. Not to himself. Not to anyone.

The album was to be called Songs in the Key of Return.

David's daughter Chloe offered to design the cover. She'd grown up around their music—quiet in the background, sketchbook always nearby. When Jonas saw her draft, he didn't change a thing. The liner notes were handwritten, scanned from a page Jonas had sent Calder late one night. A photograph from the greenroom tacked inside like an afterthought. But the release would be anything but casual. He would tap every skill he'd sharpened on the road—targeted press drops, partnered with a small distributor, embedded links inside the digital liner notes. An offering for the ones who would recognize it.

The liner note read:

> For Simon, Calder, and David. For what we carried. For what we let go.
> And for the ones still finding their way—this is for you.

Calder returned to his usual rhythm the next day—client sessions, cables, tape labels. But something in him felt newly lit. When Jonas thanked him again, he just shrugged and said, "It felt good to leave the tape running."

Jonas stayed behind a few extra days, pitching in around the studio—running cables, tuning gear, even making coffee when Calder was too deep in a mix to move. It was good work. Honest. The kind of rhythm that felt familiar in the best way. In the evenings, after the last client had packed up, they'd decompress. Swapping stories. Letting silence do the heavy lifting.

After the album was done, they booked two more sets—

not warm-ups, but quiet celebrations. They chose real rooms with real sound: one in a friend's converted loft downtown with a small stage and a board manned by someone who cared, the other at Line & Measure, a respected listening venue in the East Village, known for giving seasoned players a space to really be heard.

They invited everyone they knew. Musicians. Writers. Producers. Friends from the road. No big announcement. Just private messages, a shared sense that something worth showing up for had happened.

At Line & Measure, someone stood near the back wall, half in shadow.

He didn't speak. Didn't approach. But he listened.

Not just to the music. But to what was missing.

He slipped out before the last note rang, just as another man —unknown to Jonas—sat down near the exit, arms crossed, studying everything in silence. Their eyes met for just a moment. No words. Just a flicker of curiosity, or maybe familiarity—neither of them sure. Jonas turned away to greet someone nearby, but when he glanced back, the man was gone.

Before they packed up their gear for the last time, the band stayed out front—mingling with the crowd, shaking hands, exchanging stories.

Jonas found himself next to Simon as the last of the stragglers wandered off. For a minute they just stood there, watching the emptying space.

"I'm sorry," Jonas said. "For back then. For what Vince did, and how it ended."

Simon shrugged like it was water under a bridge. "Wasn't your fault. I stuck around longer than I should've."

Jonas shook his head. "You stayed in it."

Simon gave a small smile. "I stayed near it. Not in it. Big difference."

Jonas watched him coil a cable, no urgency in the motion. For all his years on stage, Simon had never tried to be seen. Just heard. And that, Jonas realized, was a kind of voice too.

Simon wasn't slowing down—he was heading back out on tour, playing sideman to a well-known artist with a fall schedule already filling. Still, he texted Jonas from backstage at a show in Denver: "Just sent the album to Lila Hartman. She gets it. Might reach out."

Jonas smiled when he read the name. He knew who she was— and somehow, it didn't surprise him. The right people were starting to find each other. That was the pattern. That was the sign.

After the final show, Jonas offered to drive Calder home. Tilly —the seafoam green van that had carried them so many miles —still purred to life beneath them. Jonas behind the wheel, Calder in the passenger seat. They exchanged a look and a grin, the kind only shared history could summon. Jonas gave the dash a gentle tap before turning the key. "She's still with us," he said, half to Calder, half to the van.

As they rolled north out of the city, windows cracked, silence weaving between stretches of easy conversation, both men felt the echo of those early days. Calder's place in the Hudson Valley was on the way back to Massachusetts, and Jonas didn't mind the detour. It felt right to stretch the moment a little longer.

There wasn't a plan beyond this. And maybe that was the point. The album had landed the way they'd hoped—not as a comeback, but as a confirmation. The space around Jonas didn't feel empty. It felt clear.

He didn't rush home. For the first time in a long time, he wasn't chasing something. He was listening for it.

The next morning, up at Calder's place in the Hudson Valley, he found Jonas sketching lyrics on the back of an invoice. He grinned. "You've got that look again. Just like back in the van days—when you'd start scribbling and the rest of us knew something was coming."

Jonas smiled without looking up. "Feels like something's starting to take shape."

Calder leaned in, still buzzing from the days behind the kit. "Whatever it is... don't leave me out." Jonas met his eyes and laughed. "Never again, my friend. Never again."

Then he folded the page in half and set it aside.

The work was shifting. But the rhythm remained.

Part IV: Resonance of the Voice

Every true voice finds its resonance in another.

Chapter 20 – The Album as Offering

The mornings came without urgency now.

Jonas moved through the small routines of daily life—coffee, a walk along the ridge, the slow clearing of dishes from a quiet meal alone. No alarms. No stage. But there was purpose again, just beneath the surface.

In the corner of his workspace, the worn lyric book lay open beside a checklist. Eleven songs—finalized, sequenced, and already pressed to disc. Now it was about precision: double-checking lyrics, formatting, and file alignment for the digital upload. One last pass to make sure nothing slipped out of place. There wouldn't be a do-over.

He was hearing them with wonder now—like voices he'd known by heart but only just begun to fully understand—as he followed along line by line, double-checking the lyrics against the recordings.

He sat in the stillness after the track faded. It didn't shout. But it was real.

There was something in the way they moved together. Not a formula. Not even a message. But a continuity—a sequence of waypoints for those willing to follow. They didn't explain the path. They invited it.

The song *"Happy Man,"* for instance—so deceptively lighthearted—wasn't just a confession of belief. It hinted at what he'd been taught, what he'd tried, what he wanted instead. It was a song that wove together States, Tries, Shoulds, and Desires in a way he could now see clearly.

And *"Tulips Don't Wait"*? That wasn't a poem from childhood nostalgia—it was a transmission. A pure voice of belief from a version of himself that hadn't yet been compromised.

As he revisited each track, they opened up like coded entries in a larger document.

"The Right Way" laid bare the battling forces of cultural belief systems—the Echo's demand versus the quiet clarity of the Voice.

"Don't Forget Your Dreams" reminded him why he started all of this, and why it still mattered.

"Keep On Keepin' On" pointed straight back to that same north star. "Where Did We Come From" and "The Good Life" were mythologies turned inside out. Then there was "Walk the Earth and Heaven". It carried the oldest thread of all—how early the Echo tries to rewrite us, and how vital it is to choose our own voice. And "I'm Not Free at All"—a finale for those who forget, a beginning for those who remember.

The task was nearly done—just a few details left for morning. He saved his files, stood, and stretched. The sun was starting to lower behind the ridge. His stomach growled—a quiet signal to move. The Grange potluck was calling, and he didn't need a reason to show up with his guitar. On the breeze, he caught the faintest scent of barbecue—sweet smoke and spice, the kind that made your mouth water before you even knew you were hungry.

*
**

He stepped outside into the thickening dusk. The air was warm and fragrant, still carrying the trace of barbecue from down the hill. A few birds cut quiet arcs above the trees. The road to the Grange felt familiar—not just in miles, but in rhythm. Like the kind of walk where you already know you'll be met.

He arrived just as the line for food was beginning to form, nodding a quiet hello to the cluster of volunteers near the door. A few familiar voices greeted him by name. He responded with warm smiles, light touches on shoulders, and a short laugh at someone's teasing comment about him bringing his "magic guitar." He took his time filling a plate—greeting a few more folks, trading smiles that needed no names. He'd come to recognize the rhythm of these evenings: food first, then whatever followed. He found a seat near the wall, just where he liked it—close enough to catch every detail, far enough to observe without becoming the center. For now, it was enough just to eat—something warm, something shared, something good.

That night, he brought two songs—easy and unannounced, folded into the evening like another dish at the table, their shape now part of something bigger.

First, he played "Tulips Don't Wait"—the one that started it all.

Then, "Don't Forget Your Dreams"—a reminder, for himself as much as anyone, that some promises take time, but they still matter.

As he moved into the second song, the room began to settle. The low hum of conversation faded. Forks were set down. A few people leaned back in their chairs, drawn in. It wasn't dramatic—just a quiet attunement, like the space itself had started listening.

When he finished, a hush lingered after the last note. It wasn't hesitation—it was reverence, like what they'd heard wasn't over yet. People sat still, breathing it in, as if the last note had settled somewhere deeper than sound. Then, near the back, a woman touched her chest and whispered to no one in particular, "Oh my... whatever that was... it's exactly what I needed tonight."

A soft ripple of laughter followed, gentle and knowing. The kind that said: we felt it too.

And near the edge of the folding chairs, a man with silver hair stood watching—arms crossed, chin tilted.

Jonas noticed the look. Not admiration. Something about it stirred a memory—another room, another glance, just like this. A quiet knowing. A recognition.

*
**

The last of the coffee cups were being gathered when the man with the silver hair stepped in.

"That first song," he said, nodding toward Jonas's guitar. "What was it called?"

"'Tulips Don't Wait,'" Jonas said, his voice warm.

Scott nodded slowly. "Yeah. That one hit different. It felt... like it knew something about me."

Jonas chuckled. "So what you're saying is you had a thing for talking tulips too?"

Scott laughed. "Maybe I did."

He offered a hand. "Scott Calix. I run a yoga studio over on

Laurel."

Jonas raised an eyebrow with pleasant surprise. "A yoga man. I should've guessed. You've got that grounded look."

Scott chuckled. "Took a while to earn that. I used to build enterprise systems—architecture, pipelines, performance structures. The kind of stuff that makes money flow but drains the soul."

Jonas nodded, clearly tracking. "So you've seen both sides."

Scott tilted his head nodding. "Trying to live on the one that lets people breathe."

Scott's expression shifted—more focused now. "There was something about the way those two songs sat next to each other. Like one opened a door, and the other stepped through it."

Jonas exhaled through his nose—not surprised by Scott's insight, but struck by the precision of his language. It was the second time he'd seen someone spot the pattern without being led there. First in South Carolina. Now here. Same recognition. Same pause.

"That's a good way to put it," he said.

Scott's brow furrowed, not with confusion, but curiosity. "This felt like something I'd seen before," he said, almost to himself.

"Not just two songs. Two coordinates."

He wasn't talking about his old job anymore. He was talking about pattern—the kind that tells you you're not lost, just early.

Scott leaned in slightly. "You chose those two songs on purpose, didn't you?"

Jonas nodded. "I did. I've been tracing the arc they form for a while now."

Scott went on, "They felt… linked, like one was a foundation, and the other was something you built on top of it."

"That's what they are," Jonas said. "They came from different seasons of my life, but the thread between them—it was always there. I just had to walk far enough to see it."

Scott smiled. "You gave people something real tonight. That sticks with them."

Jonas returned the smile. "I'm glad you stayed to listen."

A pause, and then: "I've already recorded them—along with the rest. Eleven in total. The final pieces just came together."

Scott's smile shifted—just slightly. A beat passed before he said,

"I was there, you know. Back at that show you did in the East Village with your band."

Jonas blinked. "You were?"

Scott nodded. "Sat in the back near the exit. Didn't say anything—just watched.

Jonas tilted his head. "So that was you."

Scott smirked. "Recognition goes both ways, doesn't it?"

He let the moment settle, then added, more thoughtfully,

"When I heard you that night in New York, I knew I'd seen something special but I didn't think I'd see you again."

He glanced around, then back to Jonas.

"And then a few months later... there you were. My town. My dinner spot."

He didn't press the meaning. He didn't have to.

Jonas held the gaze, his expression shifting—half amusement, half understanding.

"Yeah," he said. "Some threads don't need pulling. They just show up again."

Scott's smile deepened, quiet and sure.

Scott's eyes lit up. "So the album, including those two songs, is already finished?"

Jonas nodded. "The CD's in distribution. I was working on the digital upload before I came out tonight."

Jonas smiled faintly. "I'll wrap it tomorrow, after I sleep off the brisket."

Scott smiled. "A man with his priorities straight."

He leaned forward. "So then what comes next?"

Jonas paused. "That's the question, isn't it? I'm not sure yet."

Scott reached into his back pocket and pulled out a folded business card. "If you ever want to keep the thread going…"

Jonas took it without hesitation. "I will."

*
**

The next day Jonas called Scott. By early evening, they were seated across from each other at the long wooden table in Jonas's home—the same table still scattered with lyric sheets, scratch notes, and a worn-open journal.

Scott took it in slowly. The songs, the sequencing, the fragments of diagrams and marginalia—they weren't random. They were scaffolding.

"You've already outlined something bigger," Scott said, voice low with recognition. "Not just an album. A map."

He paused. "But what if this isn't just about helping people trace their way out?"

Jonas looked up.

Scott continued, "What if the real issue is—there just aren't enough songs, or stories, or voices that help people do that?"

Jonas held the gaze and blinked, the weight of the question landing without resistance. He didn't speak—just nodded, slow and sure, like someone recognizing a truth he'd almost forgotten he already knew.

Scott saw the shift—just a flicker—but enough. Enough to know the thread had landed.

He went on. "What if the system isn't for the listener... it's for the creatives who've lost the thread?"

Jonas leaned back, letting it land. "So we're not trying to teach someone how to walk the path," he said slowly. "We're trying to wake up the ones who can light the way."

Scott nodded. "Exactly. Reorient the creatives. The rest follows."

Jonas smiled. "Now that feels like something we can build."

Scott's eyes sparked. "Then let's ask the question the old system wouldn't."

Scott stood up not long after, offering a quiet goodbye. There was more to say, but not tonight. Jonas lingered in the silence after he left, the weight of their conversation still humming in the air. He looked toward the ridge, then back at the table, where the lyric sheets remained scattered like breadcrumbs.

*
**

There was an event later—one he'd marked on the calendar weeks ago. A celebration, a showcase, a small local thing. But something about it felt timely now.

Jonas arrived at the renovated arts collective just as the the presentations were getting started. The evening was part showcase, part celebration—the culmination of months of community effort to breathe new life into the space.

One of the first to present, Mira Ellison gave a fifteen-minute demonstration—part movement, part philosophical nudge—on the importance of being able to get down to and up from the floor without using your hands. Her delivery had been understated, clinical almost, but her movement spoke louder than words. Jonas hadn't been able to stop watching her—not just for what she said, but for how she embodied it.

Later, as people gathered near the buffet table and a small trio played at the far end of the hall, Jonas found her again. She stood just off-center, with a clear view of the room, posture relaxed but deliberate.

"Great talk," he said, approaching with an open smile.

She nodded, appreciative but cautious. "Thanks."

"I didn't think much about that kind of movement... until I realized how much easier it used to be for me. Back when I was living closer to the ground."

Mira glanced at him sidelong, curiosity sparked. "Living closer to the ground?"

Jonas nodded. "Van life. Campsites. Sleeping bags. You move differently when the earth is your furniture."

Mira paused, considering that for a moment. "Interesting," she said at last, then tipped her head toward the dance floor. "Tell me—what do you make of that guy's gait?"

She smiled, but a thought flickered behind it. For a moment, she assumed he was doing what she did—using questions to avoid being questioned. But something about him didn't match that pattern. His curiosity felt… untethered. Free of agenda.

Jonas followed her gaze. A middle-aged man was swaying off-beat, shoulders stiff, knees soft.

"That looks… improvised?" he offered.

Mira smirked. "Collapsed arch, overcompensating hip, probably some unresolved ankle trauma on the left side. But he's enjoying himself. That part's working fine."

Jonas laughed, delighted. "Okay, that's impressive."

She met his eyes for a beat, her eyes crinkling with quiet amusement. The moment stretched—light, unexpected, and mutual. A shared recognition, where delight answers delight.

He didn't know her in the way time allows. And yet he did—in the way the body remembers truth. Then she shrugged and said, "Patterns like that usually point to something. Once you understand what should be happening, the dysfunction becomes obvious. You can't unsee it."

They stood together like that for a while—without hurry—people-watching, analyzing movement, trading thoughts like notes in a shared sketchbook.

At one point, Jonas leaned in slightly. "Band's decent. Bass player and drummer are definitely playing some kind of game back there.

Ooo, did you catch that? Just before the transition—verse to chorus, chorus to bridge—they look at each other.

Like they know that's where things can fall apart.

But it doesn't.

And then... that little smile in their eyes—like they just landed something together."

Mira raised an eyebrow. "You know music?"

He nodded. "Used to live in it. For years, actually."

Now it was her turn. "What kind?" she asked.

"Folk, mostly. Then it got complicated. Touring. Teaching.

Writing. I stepped off the road a while back. I still play a little though—host an open mic at Sal's Pizza now and then. After potluck dinners at the Grange, sometimes I share a song or two."

She studied him a moment. Not prying—just adjusting her sense of who he might be.

She tilted her head slightly. "Do you ever miss it?"

"Sometimes," Jonas said. "But I play just enough to keep everything working. Like tuning an instrument, even if you're not planning to perform. I think I'm building something else now. Not sure what it is yet."

Mira nodded slowly. "That makes two of us."

They didn't say goodbye when they left. But as they moved through different exits into the cool night air, the same unspoken thought hovered between them:

We're going to see each other again.

On purpose.

*
**

Now, in the soft hush of evening, he sat at his kitchen table, fingers wrapped around a warm mug. The upload was done. Now came the wait—not for applause, but for the silent gears of the system to finish turning. What settled in him wasn't closure. It was the feeling of anticipating connection.

He was following a thread—something that had started with a conversation about systems and stretched through the way Mira had read a stranger's gait like sheet music. Not answers. Just alignments.

He thought back to what Scott had said the night before. Not just a map for the lost, but a signal for those who could help others find their way. That thought was still echoing, looping in his chest like a refrain.

*
**

Across town, Scott stood in front of the whiteboard. He hadn't used it in weeks—not since the last workshop at the studio. But tonight, he picked up the pen without hesitation. No diagrams. No flowcharts. Just a sweeping curve, open-ended, like a path arcing toward possibility.

Beside it, he wrote two words:

entry point.

And beneath that, almost as an afterthought—but maybe it was the heart of the whole thing—he added:

for the creatives.

*
**

And in her quiet space lit by early evening light, Mira

replayed a moment from the party in her head—Jonas's comment about the rhythm between the bass player and drummer. It stayed with her. The way he noticed things, the way he asked. It was about more than music.

She scribbled a note in the margin of her presentation draft: Stability isn't stillness. It's timing. Or maybe it's timing that makes stability feel like flow.

None of them called each other. No one made a plan.

But the next step had already begun.

*
**

That morning, Jonas heard the soft ping of a notification.

The processing was complete. The songs—long carried, slowly clarified—were now delivered to the world's digital shelves. Not launched. Not promoted. Just… available.

Jonas sat for a while and stared at the screen in the stillness. Not out of nostalgia. Just to notice what this moment was. Not a finish line. Not a beginning.

It wasn't just a project. It was a remembering.

It felt like the first fruit of a seed planted long ago—finally ripened, not for display, but for offering.

A continuation.

A returning.

He stood slowly, mug in hand, and looked out toward the ridge. The light was already reaching past the tallest branches. He felt it in his chest—like an extra beat, quiet and sure, as if the Voice itself had nodded back.

He took a slow sip from the mug, savoring the warmth more than the taste. Then he turned, walked back to the table, and sat down.

All that was left now was to use the systems he'd developed over years of touring—email templates, segmented lists, venue archives, in one lovingly cobbled-together CRM—Jonas prepared the announcement. No PR. No press. Just a direct note to the people who had walked pieces of the path with him.

The subject line read:

"Songs in the Key of Return — Not a product. A mirror. A map. A memory."

The message was short:

"This is not a relaunch, a rebrand, or a return to.

These songs are a reflection—of what was seen, what was asked, and what endured.

Nothing that doesn't matter, no packaging, no merch. Just songs that belong together, right here.

"If they speak to you, they're yours.

And if you were part of this road—at any point, in any way—thank you. This wouldn't exist without you."

Stream "Songs in the Key of Return" here. Simple. Accessible. Sustainable.

Yours truly, Jonas

*
**

A few minutes later, he heard a knock—Scott had taken him up on his invitation to hang out after the launch.

By early evening, they were sitting at the kitchen table when the first responses began to roll in. Emails. Messages. Comments on old posts he'd forgotten were still up. Virtual applause from listeners scattered across years and miles—people who'd seen him in dim cafes, bookstores, open-air stages, and student union halls. People who remembered his voice and found something of themselves in these recorded versions.

*
**

In a quiet apartment two time zones away, Vince clicked the link without hesitation.

He'd been at Line & Measure that night. No one saw him.

But he saw everything—the crowd, the stillness, the way Jonas played like nothing was missing.

The songs said what needed saying. And for the first time in years, Vince heard Jonas without defensiveness, without noise.

He wasn't angry anymore.

After the final track, he just sat there—longer than he expected.

He didn't think he was going to reply.

But after sitting with it a while, he typed out one line and hit send:

"Not the ending I caused. I see the thread you followed. And I respect it."

He read Vince's message once, then again.

Not surprised. Not bitter. Just… grateful.

Vince had always been near the signal.

Now, at least once, he'd heard it clearly.

And that was enough.

*
**

And in a second-floor walk-up above a bookstore in Manhattan, Isabel let the final track linger. She hadn't expected to feel anything. But when it ended, she closed her laptop and sat still for a long moment.

She whispered thank you—not to Jonas, but to the version of herself that once believed they could change the world together. And she knew now: maybe they had. Just not in the way she thought.

Then, without a greeting, she sent:

"After I left that life—the rhythm, the road, the Voice—I landed somewhere I thought I could manage. But it was a place where everything around me made it easy to forget.
Easy to choose comfort over what we'd seen.
And I did. I didn't mean to, but I did.
I shut the door on something we both knew.
But I'm starting to remember.
And the window's open again."

He read her words slowly —

not once, but twice.

Then he sat back and exhaled—

not with pride, but with relief.

This was Isabel.

He'd seen it in the man at the coffeehouse in South Carolina.

He'd seen it at the Grange.

And now—

the thread, still alive,

pulling her gently back...

remembering something she once knew...the Voice.

After those two came the rest—less tangled in the story, but no less moved by the songs.

Some wrote full paragraphs. Others sent a single line.

"I didn't know how much I needed this until now."

"You've still got it."

"This feels like closure... and a beginning for me."

Scott read them all quietly. Not intruding. Just witnessing.

When Jonas turned to him, unread messages still filling the corner of the screen, Scott didn't offer a summary or an assessment.

He just nodded and said, "You just made room for what's next."

Jonas smiled.

He knew it too.

Scott stood soon after, offering a quiet goodbye. The weight of the evening still hung between them, but the thread would hold until next time.

Later that night, across town, Scott closed his laptop but didn't move. He let the silence linger, listening not to the music, but to the echoes of the responses. He hadn't built Jonas's album, but he felt its architecture. It was clean. It shimmered.

He looked over at the whiteboard—still bearing the curve he'd drawn the week before. Beside it were the words he'd written in two parts:

entry point

for the creatives

He picked up the marker and, beneath them, added one more:

awakening.

*
**

Elsewhere, Mira sat on her front steps, scrolling through her phone. She hadn't searched Jonas by name, not exactly. But the algorithm had helped her along.

A link appeared—an album drop, "Songs in the Key of Return"…a Jonas Wilder offering. She smiled—of course it found her. Then she tapped.

Headphones in, she listened. Not passively. Not professionally. Just… listened.

Halfway through the second track, she paused and jotted a

note on the back of a grocery list:

"Movement keeps the instrument tuned."

She looked at the note, then at the night sky, and smiled slightly.

She didn't follow him. Didn't message. Just kept listening.

The next step was still unspoken.

But it was already in motion.

Chapter 21 – What Was Meant to Be Found

The letter arrived on a Tuesday. An Indiana return address, a looping script Jonas didn't recognize. But the name—Connie Wilder—gave him pause.

Aunt Connie? After all these years? He hadn't seen her since the only Wilder family reunion he ever attended. He was thirteen. A sunny afternoon filled with smiles and small talk, cousins running through sprinklers, uncles nursing beers. On the surface, it looked like any other family. But underneath, there were fractures—old rifts, unspoken wounds. His father, the eldest of five, was the most emotionally distant of them all.

Connie, though—he remembered her. Warm, funny, quick to listen. She'd made him laugh once with a story about his dad as a teenager, and it stuck with him. He never saw her again after that day. But now, holding her letter, he could feel it—she had been paying attention all along.

Inside the envelope was a handwritten note from Connie, a photograph of a young man in uniform with Jonas's eyes, and a yellowed page of lined paper.

* * *

Dear Jonas,

I don't know if you remember me, but I remember you—quiet, thoughtful, and watching the world with eyes older than your age. That reunion feels like a lifetime ago, but I still remember you laughing at that story I told about your dad trying to drive a tractor in reverse. It stuck with me.

A friend sent me your album last month. I wasn't sure what to expect—but the moment I heard your voice, something inside me stopped. Not just because it was good (it is), but because I heard someone else in there too. Your grandfather. There's a tone he used to carry—honest, searching. It's in you. I think he'd be proud. I know I was moved.

That's when I knew why I'd held onto this letter. I never quite knew what to do with it when your father refused it. But now, I think it was meant to find its way to you when the time was right.

All is well on my end. My youngest just started working with AmeriCorps, and we're all figuring out this strange new world one day at a time.

I hope you're safe and well. Stay in touch if you ever feel like it.

With love,

Connie

The page she enclosed smelled of cedar and time. Jonas unfolded it with reverence. The ink had faded, the script shaky and deliberate:

"When I was young, I believed I was meant to write songs. To tell stories. To make something true. Then came the war. And when I returned, everything was louder—expectations, survival, the American dream. I stopped singing. I stopped listening. I traded truth for comfort. And it cost me everything."

Jonas read the last line again: "I traded truth for comfort. And it cost me everything."

His throat tightened. The words echoed—exactly—from a dream he'd had the night before he dropped out of college. In the dream, he'd stood face-to-face with a man he didn't know, asking:

"Who are you?"

The man didn't answer. He simply said:

"Constance has something for you."

Back then, Jonas hadn't known what that meant. The name Constance hadn't registered. He hadn't even known that was his aunt's full name.

But now—holding the paper, reading the words from the man in his dream, delivered by the woman he knew only as Aunt Connie—he understood. The dream hadn't come from nowhere. Whether it rose from his own subconscious or from something deeper—older—it had carried truth. These weren't just imagined. They were inherited messages.

One man couldn't carry it. One family couldn't hold it. The failure of love was only the shadow of silence—born from forgetting something older, quieter, and real.

He thought of his father. His grandfather. Himself. Then

everyone else—millions shaped by noise—poured into the space hollowed by silence." So many never knowing what they'd lost... only that something was missing.

This time, the thread hadn't vanished. It had led here. And now, it had work to do.

Not just to help someone remember—but to help someone else help them remember.

That's how the voice becomes a bridge back home.

*
**

He sat down at the small kitchen table when a knock at the side door broke the quiet. It was Scott, smiling and carrying two coffees. But something in Jonas's stillness caught him, and his smile softened—a quiet shift into a look that said he knew it was time to listen instead of ask.

They sat outside on the back steps, the late afternoon sun slanting low behind the trees. For a while, neither spoke.

After a long silence, Jonas said quietly, "I got a letter this morning. From my aunt. It had a note my grandfather wrote before he died."

Scott didn't say anything, just looked at him.

Jonas went on, "Turns out... I wasn't the first in my family to hear it. My grandfather did, once. Then he lost it. Regretted it.

And somehow... even through all that silence, his message still made its way here."

Scott took that in. "That's heavy."

"No," Jonas said. "It's clarifying." He looked out at the trees. "It was a reminder that it's not about passing something down the right way. It's about what happens when it gets lost —and what it takes for someone to find it again."

He paused, then added, "I used to think my father chose silence. But now I see—he just didn't know how to find the thread again. It had already slipped too far from reach."

Scott nodded slowly. "Knowing where his silence came from —that must be a kind of relief."

"It is," Jonas said. "I made peace with it a long time ago. But this—this just confirms what we already sensed. That the silence isn't personal—it's structural. And the work we're doing? It pushes back."

He glanced at Jonas again, sensing the weight had shifted —like something unspoken had settled into place.

"I've been thinking about our last conversation," he said.

Jonas turned, a small smile forming. "Me too."

Scott took a breath. "What we left hanging was this: if we can reorient the creatives—the ones who've lost the thread—

maybe the rest will follow."

Jonas nodded. "Right, and to do that, we have to ask a different question. One the old system never could."

Scott looked out toward the trees. "Because if we don't, the forgetting continues. And too many people never find what was meant for them to recover."

They sat with it as a breeze stirred the leaves—like the trees themselves had been listening. The silence between them wasn't empty—it glowed faintly, like something had just been struck and was waiting to catch.

Scott stood, brushing off his hands. "We should meet tomorrow," he said. "Talk it through. That thought deserves a good night's sleep."

Jonas nodded. "Bring the notebook."

"I will," Scott said. "And a few quiet hours."

He didn't linger. Just gave a knowing nod and disappeared down the path, the day's last light stretching long across the ground.

Chapter 22 – The Invitation

The next morning was overcast, the kind of quiet sky that made everything feel like it was listening.

Jonas set two mugs on the table and opened the window a crack. The smell of pine drifted in. He didn't write anything down. Just waited.

Scott arrived right on time, a slim notebook under one arm, his usual energy dialed low and focused. He didn't need instructions. He just sat, opened the notebook, and looked across the table.

Then Scott said, "You ready?"

Jonas nodded. "You?"

Scott offered the smallest of smiles. "Let's start with what this really is. An entry point—for the creatives. And if we get it right, a spark for awakening."

Jonas exhaled. "Because people are collapsing midstream. Midlife. Mid-song. And they don't even know why."

Scott didn't interrupt. He let the shape of that sentence hang a little longer.

Jonas went on. "They think it's failure. Or aging. Or some

mistake they made. But really… it's disconnection. They've lost the thread. And no one ever told them there was a thread to begin with."

Scott nodded, scribbled something.

"We're not trying to fix them," Jonas added. "We're trying to offer a way back to something they forgot they even had."

Scott looked up. "So the invitation isn't about telling anyone what's broken. It's about asking the people who can make something—the creatives—to point toward what's possible."

Jonas lifted his mug. "Exactly."

Scott flipped to a clean page.

"I've been playing with a line that might be a starting point," he said, and started writing.

> What would you make if you trusted someone else was
> waiting for it?

He turned the notebook around.

Jonas read it. Shook his head, not in dismissal but with a kind of patient precision.

"It's not wrong," he said. "But it's still assuming awareness. That someone's waiting. Most people aren't. They're numb. They don't even know they're missing anything."

Scott nodded slowly. "Right. So let's take the burden off the receiver."

He crossed out a few words and began again.

What would you make if you knew someone needed it—even

if they didn't know it yet?

Jonas studied it.

"Closer," he said. "But maybe we can get even tighter. Less about what they don't know. More about what the creatives of the world can help them remember."

Scott smiled. "Go on."

Jonas leaned forward, then said it aloud, slowly, testing the balance of it.

"What would you make if you knew it might help someone remember they had a choice?"

Scott stopped writing. Looked up.

There was a stillness in the room, not empty but charged.

"That's it," he said quietly. "That's the one."

Scott wrote it down and then underlined the question.

"That's the thread," he said. "Now let's invite them to pick it up."

He turned the page and began again—this time writing the message they'd send:

An invitation: What would you make if you knew it might help someone remember they had a choice?

No pitch. No program. Just a time, a place, and a space to bring what matters. Something to offer. Something to share.

If you've crossed paths with Jonas—maybe heard him at the Grange, or seen him at the open mic—then you already know: it's not about performance. It's about remembering.

We'd love for you to listen to his latest album before you come. We're not gathering to discuss it—we're gathering to make something new. But a thread starts there.

Because someone, somewhere, is closer to remembering than they know.

He opened his laptop. Typed it out exactly as written. Then paused, finger hovering over the "send" button.

Jonas watched him. "What's wrong, cold feet?"

Scott chuckled. "Nah. Just counting it in."

He clicked. The message went out.

They didn't celebrate. Just traded a grin over their mugs and let the silence hum.

Jonas looked out the window.

"That didn't feel like sending something," he said. "It felt like lighting something."

Scott nodded.

"That's the point."

Chapter 23 – The First Chord

The sun hadn't yet cleared the ridge line when Jonas stepped out barefoot onto the dewy grass, coffee in hand, notebook under one arm. The quiet here was different—less like the absence of sound and more like the presence of listening. He walked slowly toward the edge of the field where the trees began, letting the rhythm of his footsteps settle something inside him.

He traced the thread he'd been following back through time—the letter from his grandfather, the making of the album, the fallout with Vince. Even further.

He thought back to the night in South Carolina. A small room, folding chairs, scuffed wood floor. A man seated with his daughters, listening—and then something shifted. The man hadn't just heard the song. He had been changed by it.

Jonas no longer needed to replay the details to understand. The meaning was in what followed: the man's letter. The quiet revolution. The transformation that wasn't loud, but real. And lasting.

That was the proof. Not because the world was listening.

But because one person had.

That night had marked the beginning of a new kind of clarity. Not the electrified kind that fuels ambition, but the grounded kind that points to something steady. Something that mattered.

His father had never taught him to listen for that. His grandfather, as Jonas now understood, hadn't forgotten by accident—but under the pressure of survival, of noise, of trading truth for comfort.

Forgetting belongs to the past. What matters now is the path we offer others—to remember.

Jonas sat on the low stone wall at the edge of the clearing and opened his notebook. He didn't write much—just a line he'd been circling around for days:

Don't ask what you want to say. Ask what someone needs to remember.

He underlined it once, then closed the book and sat still, letting the morning come up around him.

*
**

Just beyond the studio, a simple open stretch of land Scott used before for outdoor sessions—trees marking the edges, sky overhead, nothing fancy.

They hadn't done much to prepare it. A circle of folding

chairs and woven blankets, a few rough-cut logs for sitting or leaning against, and a makeshift table with a thermos of coffee and a stack of paper cups. No microphone. No agenda posted. Just a hand-painted sign at the entrance:

"What would you make
if you knew it might help someone
remember they had a choice?"

Guests began to arrive in ones and twos. Some came with sketchbooks tucked under their arms, others with instruments slung over shoulders. There were dancers and dreamers, a playwright, a retired teacher, a high school kid whose mother had driven her an hour to be there.

They didn't all arrive with the same understanding. Some had received the invitation directly, the question already etched into their minds. Others came because someone they trusted had said, *"You need to be here,"* and only saw the question for the first time on the sign at the entrance.

Some had listened to the album beforehand—and stepped into the space already marked by its quiet clarity. Others came with no more than a hunch, a tug, a willingness to follow what called them.

But no one knew exactly what they were stepping into. That, at least, was universal. And still—they had made space for this.

Mira moved among them quietly, offering smiles, nods, and mugs of coffee. She didn't need to say much. Her presence did the welcoming.

Scott adjusted a chair, checked the thermos, nodded to Jonas. No speech, no call to attention. Just a slow, organic gathering.

When the last guest settled, Jonas stepped forward—not onto a stage, but simply into the center of the circle. His voice was calm.

"We're not here to teach," he said. "We're here because we've been working on something—and we need your help."

He paused, letting the words land.

"This isn't a workshop. It's a beginning."

*

Jonas didn't launch into a speech. He glanced at Scott, then back at the circle.

A little over a year ago, I was standing in a room not too different from this—except smaller, darker, and with worse coffee.

It was supposed to be just another show. But after I played a few songs, something happened.

A man came up to me afterward and said, 'I don't know what's happening to me, but I think I've been asleep most of my life.'

He let the sentence rest.

"That wasn't the first time someone had said something like that. But it was the first time I believed it had something to do with me. He wasn't responding to me. He was responding to something in himself. Something the music had uncovered."

Jonas looked down for a moment, then back up.

"I wrote that album over a long stretch of time, trying to make sense of the world I was moving through. I didn't have much of a plan, but I was listening—to the silence between things. That's where the songs came from."

Scott stepped forward then, picking up the thread without ceremony.

"Funny thing—I saw Jonas play once, way before we actually met. A show in the East Village with his band. I was way in the back. Didn't say a word. I didn't even know what I was seeing at the time... just that it reached me. Got under my skin."

He glanced down, then back at the group.

"And then a couple weeks later, I walk into my usual dinner place—and there he is again. Different setting, same presence. The whole room felt it."

He ran a hand through his hair, exhaling softly—still caught in the weight of it.

"After dinner I introduced myself and we started to talk—and that's when I learned about the album. When I listened to it, I wasn't just listening—I was seeing it. Not as a tracklist, but as a kind of map. One that pointed away from performance and toward something else."

"That's when I knew meeting Jonas wasn't a coincidence. The songs weren't just songs. They were coordinates."

Jonas added, his voice almost a whisper.

"Coordinates... but not for finding. For remembering. Something older. Something quieter."

Scott nodded.

"What struck me was how the songs held together—not by style or theme, but by what they resisted. They weren't trying to fix

anything. They were refusing to pretend that nothing needed fixing. And that refusal? That was the signal."

He turned back to the group.

"That's why we're here. Because that kind of refusal is rare—and it's powerful. But it's also not enough on its own. It needs to become part of something. Something we can build with. Maybe even something we've already begun."

He paused, just long enough for the quiet to settle again. Scott finished the thought, his voice low.

"That's what we've been working on. And this—" he gestured gently toward the circle "—is where it begins."

*
**

Scott stayed standing, but shifted his stance—less presentation now, more presence. His voice matched it.

"We're not here to talk about songs," We're here because something about the way we live—our systems, our structures —has been flattening us for generations. Making us forget we were ever meant to be whole."

No one looked away. The group had settled into a kind of

listening that didn't need explanation.

"We've learned to function in systems that expect results and conformity. But not meaning. Not connection. Not what makes us feel alive. The cost of that has been mounting since the beginning of what we call progress. Those of us who've been watching... we've felt it. Seen it. In ourselves. In the work. In the world."

He paused, then turned to Jonas with a quiet nod.

"You told me a story once, about a roadside stop. A man and his daughters. A song that changed something."

Jonas didn't shift. He just let the memory rise.

"It wasn't dramatic. He didn't cry or stand up or interrupt. He just... stilled. Like something once buried had lifted. It wasn't a single lyric. It was the way the songs sequenced—each one unlocking a little more—until he remembered he still had a choice."

He glanced at the group, then back at Scott.

"Afterward, he waited until his family had gone. He walked up to me while I was wrapping cables. He looked a little unsettled,

but clear in some new way. All he said was, 'I don't know what's happening to me, but I think I've been asleep most of my life."

Jonas let that settle before adding,

"It didn't surprise me that it happened. Just when. I saw it for what it was right away—a remembering, not a discovery."

Scott turned to the group again, voice low but sure.

"That's the point. That kind of response... that's the compass. It's not applause. It's not conversion. It's a shift back to all. A remembering."

The breeze picked up slightly, lifting the corner of a notebook in someone's lap.

Jonas stepped forward again, his tone quiet but clear.

We're not trying to define the system. Or even dismantle it. But we can see what it's done to us—not just as individuals, but as a people. And we can respond by making things that help others remember they were never without a choice.

Starting here. Starting now.

*
**

For a moment, no one spoke. The stillness wasn't awkward—

it felt earned.

Jonas let the quiet linger before stepping forward again.

"When I first started writing songs, I thought I could change the world with one. A lot of us do."

A few soft nods, knowing smiles.

"But what I've come to understand is that it's not that simple. If a song has the power to change anything, it's only because it came from someplace deeper—downstream from listening. Not listening to noise or opinion—but to the thing beneath it all. The part that hasn't gone silent, just unheard."

His gaze moved slowly around the circle.

"That's what I've been learning to do. What we've been learning to do. Listen—not just for what we want to say, but for what someone might need to hear – to remember."

He let the line land. A beat passed.

"That's why we're here."

He looked at Scott, then stepped back.

Scott took a breath, then added,

"We're not trying to fix culture with content. We're trying to diversify what content is for."

The circle felt different now. Not larger—but deeper.

Jonas finished the thought, voice steady.

"To reorient the arts—not toward more noise, but toward what matters most to us. As people. As a culture. As the collective we call humanity."

He didn't offer a call to action. He didn't need to.

*
**

Scott looked out at the group, then spoke simply.

"So... What would you make if you knew it might help someone remember they had a choice?"

No flourish. Just the question, placed gently back in their hands.

For a moment, there was only the sound of wind moving through the trees.

Then Mira shifted forward, elbows resting lightly on her knees.

"I think I'd start with the body, voice calm but sure. "Not to

perform with it—but to listen through it. To help people feel where they've gone numb. Maybe that's a good first remembering."

No one interrupted. The silence made room for her words to keep echoing.

Across the circle, a woman with silver-streaked hair and faded paint smudges on her sleeves spoke next.

"I've had this idea for years," she said. "A theater project—for kids. Not to teach them how to act, but to let them act out different versions of their lives. To explore choices they didn't know they had. To feel, in their bodies, what it might be like to become someone else—maybe even someone freer."

She glanced down, then back up.

"I think... if even one of them remembered they had a choice, that their story wasn't already written—then it would be worth it."

A few heads nodded. Someone scribbled something in the margin of their notebook.

Someone near the back shifted. A man in his thirties, hoodie sleeves pushed up to his elbows, spoke—softly, like he wasn't sure he was allowed to.

"But what if I don't get it right? What if I try… and it doesn't help anyone remember anything?"

He looked down, then up.

"What if I'm not the one they need to hear it from?"

The words landed and stayed—like a ripple across still water. Around the circle, eyes softened. Shoulders shifted. The question wasn't his—it was everyone's. Spoken by one voice, but felt in every chest.

For a moment, no one responded. Then, from the far side of the circle, a quiet motion.

A hand raised. Small, tentative. Like in a classroom.

Scott noticed first, nodded gently. "Go ahead."

It was the high school girl—quiet until now, her mother sitting just behind her. She looked around, then spoke. Her voice was soft, but clear.

"Maybe it's not about being the one," she said. "Maybe it's just about being someone who's listening. If you start there… I don't think you can get it wrong."

She didn't look away. Her gaze found his, steady and soft, and she gave a small, almost imperceptible nod—like she wanted him to know he'd been heard.

The silence that followed wasn't heavy—it was reverent.

Even Jonas blinked, like something in him had just been reset.

The room held still—not frozen, but full. Like something real had just shifted its weight to make room for more.

*
**

Jonas didn't say anything. He didn't need to. He just sat quietly, hands resting on his knees, watching the circle—not as a leader, but as a witness.

Someone adjusted a blanket. A bird called out once, then again. The embers in the fire pit cracked softly, then fell still.

No one moved to leave.

It wasn't a pause waiting to be broken. It was a stillness with weight. Like the air itself had thickened with meaning—something that had passed among them not in words, but in willingness.

Jonas glanced at Scott—just briefly. A small look of quiet thanks, shared without words.

This was the moment they'd hoped for. Not applause. Not answers.

Just a pattern, beginning to ripple.

Then, from the edge of the circle, a voice—older, quiet, almost to themselves, but clear enough to carry.

"Imagine if there were thousands of people doing this."

Jonas smiled. ""That's the invitation, isn't it?"

A beat later, the girl's voice again—gentle and sure.

"Then yes. Let's."

She looked toward Jonas.

"There's another gathering, isn't there? At the Arts Collective?"

Scott answered softly,

"There is."

She nodded once.

"Good. We'll need more chairs."

That was all.

The circle held—and widened.

And the morning kept unfolding.

*
**

Later, once the last mugs were gathered and the circle had thinned into pairs walking slowly toward their cars, Jonas lingered at the edge of the field. He didn't need to be alone. But he needed a moment.

The air still carried it—that low hum of something not finished, only paused. He pulled out his phone, thumb hovering for a second before opening a group thread: Simon, Calder, David.

He typed:

"Tonight felt different. Not big. Not loud. Just true."

He paused. A breath. Then:

"We're continuing it next month. Same time, Arts Collective this time. No stage. Just a circle. If it's in you to come—bring it!
"You're part of this already. Remember, showing up—that's how we found each other. That's how the ones who come next will know where to begin."

Another line, unedited:

"A high school girl lit up the circle like she's been waiting her whole life to say what no one else could. I think she might name the whole next chapter if she has the chance."

Then, the last thought:

"Whatever lives in us that still wants to build something

better... I think it just got called forward. Let's not leave it hanging."

He hit send.

No expectation. No read receipts needed.

The first chord was in the air—not just sound, but signal.

Chapter 24 – Voices from the Circle

The light had just begun to shift—the kind of golden haze that made everything feel touched by invitation. Through the wide front windows of the arts collective, you could see movement inside: cushions being adjusted, wires tucked away, fresh art hung just hours ago. A piano waited in the corner like it knew its time would come.

Jonas arrived early, not because he needed to prepare anything—he wasn't leading tonight—but because something in him wanted to see the room before it filled. A few volunteers greeted him with warm nods and quiet hands busy with final details. He offered to help move a table but was gently waved off. *"Just be here, Jonas"* someone said. *"That's more than enough."*

Along the far wall, Mira was unrolling mats in a curved formation, like ripples from a dropped stone. She placed a tidy stack of "Swimming in Gravity" cards on a low bench nearby. Her movements were slow, efficient, present—each gesture already an invitation to drop in.

The front doors opened again. Simon entered, guitar case

in one hand, a second bag slung over his shoulder. At his side walked Lila Hartman. Her hair was pinned back loosely, her presence quiet but unmistakable. She took in the space with a single glance, then met Jonas's eyes. No words—just recognition. The kind that says, *I see what this is. I'm here because I see it.*

They embraced briefly, and it didn't matter that this was the first time they'd met in person. Some currents didn't need a history to be real.

David Manolis and Calder Chase arrived moments later. Calder carried his djembe like luggage he never put down. *"You never know when the spirit's gonna need percussion,"* he quipped, bumping fists with Simon and giving Jonas a one-armed hug.

By now, the room was beginning to pulse with bodies and breath. Friends of the collective, curious locals, and wide-eyed teens filtering in from Anaya's school, who had heard something was happening but didn't know what it was. Some carried sketchbooks. Some wore earbuds, half-disconnected until the atmosphere pulled them in.

No one announced that it was beginning.

But it was.

*
**

The murmur of conversation softened as Scott stepped gently into the center of the room. No mic. No agenda. Just presence. "Welcome," he said simply, his voice carrying without effort. "Before anything else, Mira's going to open something for us. It's not a performance—it's a pathway."

He stepped aside. Mira took his place, barefoot now, her palms open.

"For those of you willing and able," she said, "we'll begin on the ground. Find a spot. Lie down. Let gravity take the lead."

There was a moment of hesitation—then motion. People shifted, stretched, settled. Cushions, mats, coats folded beneath heads. The room recalibrated itself, becoming horizontal.

Mira knelt among them, her voice low and fluid.

"Let the back of your body meet the floor. Not as surrender. As collaboration."

"This floor isn't holding you up. It's a collaborator helping you learn how to listen from the inside."

"You're swimming in gravity now. It moves through you. It speaks through sensation."

She walked slowly between the forms, not instructing, just evoking.

"This is where you can begin to hear what's always been there. You just haven't been taught to listen."

The room exhaled as one. Breath deepened. Faces softened. The tension of arrival gave way to something else—an unspoken permission to simply be.
Even the watchers—those who didn't lie down—felt it. Mira wasn't teaching. She was remembering something out loud.
After several minutes, she whispered,

"Take your time. When you're ready, return upright. But bring the memory of your relationship to the floor with you."

The silence that followed wasn't awkward. It was awake.

⁎⁎

As bodies returned upright, some cross-legged, some leaning back on their hands, there was a subtle shift. The kind that happens when people stop waiting for the night to begin— and realize it already has.
Jonas and Scott stepped forward—not to present, but to mark a thread.

Jonas began, his voice thoughtful, a little rough from not speaking much yet tonight.

"This didn't start with a plan. It started with a question I couldn't shake. It kept showing up in different forms, but it always pointed back to the same thing."

Scott picked up the thread without pause, like they'd done this before.

"Most organizations fail because they're still asking the same questions that created the problem."

He looked out across the room.

"So we tried different questions."

Jonas nodded.

"First it was: What would you make if you trusted someone else was waiting for it?"
A few people in the room stirred, hearing the echo from a previous circle.

Scott continued, a wry smile at the corner of his mouth.

"Then it became: What would you make if you knew someone

needed it—even if they didn't know it yet?"

Jonas took a breath.

"And finally—at least for now—we arrived here: What would you make if you knew it might help someone remember they had a choice?"

There was no applause. No explanation. Just a kind of pause that respected what had just been named.

Scott looked around the room and said, "That question's not here to be answered tonight. It's here to open something. And as you'll see in a moment—some already have."

They stepped back. The floor belonged to everyone now.

*
**

No formal announcement marked the shift. The room simply quieted as Anaya Pierce stepped into the circle, her spine straight, her voice clear.

"This next piece was made by a few of us from school. It's called From Conflict to Connect. It doesn't have answers. But it has a question."

Beside her stood Ava Ramirez, grounded as ever, offering a soft nod of encouragement but letting the teens take the space.

Three young performers entered, forming a triangle: one turned away, one coiled tight, one trying to reach.

There was no dialogue at first. Just breath and movement —shoulders rising, arms flinching, feet shifting backwards. The triangle tightened. The tension grew.

Suddenly a voice cut through, not shouted but audible:

"You don't listen."

Another:

"You always need to be right."

The third, softly:

"You said it didn't matter."

Each line fell heavy, not just in what it said, but what it left unsaid.

The next beat opened into a slow unraveling. Each teen took a single step forward, not toward each other—but toward the center. Toward a question.

Then silence.

One of them knelt.

Another sat beside them.

The last joined without looking.

They spoke in unison:

"What would it take to connect?"

No resolution. No tidy ending. Just the image of three young bodies breathing together in the middle of a room full of people who suddenly remembered how hard—and brave—it was to ask that out loud.

Anaya didn't step back in. She simply returned to her seat.

Ava walked forward only to say, "They made this in two afternoons. No director. Just lived experience—and the courage to ask questions most people avoid."

There was a moment of stillness—acknowledging what had just been shared.

Then Scott stepped forward.

"If you're carrying a seed, speak it, someone here might be holding your missing piece."

*
**

There was no emcee. Just an opening—and someone stepped into it.

From the edge of the circle, a woman stood. Mid-sixties, silver braid down her back, holding a small tri-fold storyboard made from construction paper. She stepped into the space slowly and turned it toward the room and spoke , her voice clear but unpracticed.

"It's not finished, but this is the children's play I've been dreaming about for years. It's called The Bridge with No Name. Every scene ends with a choice that the audience gets to change the next night."

She handed it to someone nearby.

"Pass it around if you want. Or don't. I just needed to let it out of the drawer."

Someone across the room cued up an audio note on their phone. A teen boy—maybe sixteen, hoodie pulled halfway over his face—raised the device and hit play.
A voice filled the room. Cracking. Raw.

"Sometimes I think the only way I'll matter is if I make everyone else happy first."

The monologue rolled on for just over a minute. Honest. Rough-edged. Beautiful.

When it ended, he didn't look up. Just slid the phone back into his pocket and melted into the group again.

Mira stepped forward next—not to teach, but to offer. She held up a small stack of palm-sized cards.

"If something moved in you during the floor work, I wrote down a few reminders you can take with you. They're not instructions. Just invitations."

She placed them gently on a low table near the window, beside a handmade sign that read:

THE BLUEPRINT TABLE

Leave something. Read something. Ask someone about theirs.

A few people wandered over, quietly. Nothing orchestrated. Just the slow forming of things shared.

***

It started with a voice from somewhere near the back.

"Hey—can we hear Keep on Keepin' On?"

A few cheers followed, like someone had cracked the seal on a shared thought.

Jonas scanned the room—David was already moving toward the piano. "Been waiting for someone to ask," he said, sliding onto the bench.

Simon pulled his guitar around. Calder gave a little whoop and dropped his djembe between his knees.

"I got a groove for that one," he grinned. "Always did."

Lila raised her eyebrows in amused approval. "Well... now it's a party."

Jonas chuckled as he stepped forward.

"This one's not subtle," he said. "But maybe tonight doesn't call for subtle."

He looked over at Calder, who set the tempo with a four-count head bob. Jonas hit the opening riff with confidence, and Simon and Calder dropped in—driving it forward. The kind of rhythm that made even the back row sit up straighter. Jonas let the beat carry him into the first lines:

Time goes by...
The race goes on...
There's something about a dream...
That makes you carry on...

The words landed different tonight. Not as nostalgia—but as momentum.

By the time they hit the chorus, David dropped in on piano and the crowd was with them:

Keep on keepin' on,
Never give up the fight...

Lila, still seated, picked up the chorus in harmony, her voice threading around Jonas's like a familiar memory.

Other voices joined in, some knowing the lyrics, others faking their way into it with joy. Feet tapped. Shoulders swayed. A few teens stood up instinctively, like their bodies knew how to answer even before their minds caught up.

The song didn't end so much as crest. The final chord held like a ribbon tossed in the air—looping once before settling down.

It took only a beat before the room answered back—clapping, whooping, stomping along the floorboards. It wasn't the ending they were clapping for. It was the arrival of something they'd all helped make.

*
**

As the last note settled, the energy in the room didn't drop—it shifted. From shared movement to quiet presence. From chorus to conversation.

Scott stepped forward again—not to close the night, but to open it further.

"If something moved in you, don't wait. Speak it. You might be holding someone else's missing piece."

He didn't linger. Just that.

And somehow, it was enough.

A young woman in the back turned to the person beside her and said,

"I've been writing something. I think it's a poem. I don't know. It might be a scene."

Someone else said,

"I've had a project I've been sitting on for six years. I didn't know anyone would care."

A sketchpad was passed. A phone shared. A soft laugh in one corner, a quiet cry in another.

Near the window, someone picked up a "Swimming in Gravity" card and slid it into their pocket without reading it. They just... knew.

The room had become a current—small eddies forming, drifting, converging. Nothing forced. Nothing claimed.

Just movement.

Just return.

*
**

The room hadn't emptied entirely, but the circle had thinned. A few people lingered near the Blueprint Table. Someone was quietly collecting cushions. A guitar hummed its last vibration as it was zipped back into its case.

Jonas sat near the corner window, legs stretched out in front of him, back resting against the wall. Lila had joined him, her knees drawn up, arms resting loosely. Simon leaned against the piano bench, half-turned toward them, still barefoot.

No one spoke at first.

Then Lila broke the silence.

"No one pitched anything," she said, "but I've never seen so many ideas trying to be born."

Jonas let out a laugh and shook his head, grinning wide.

"I know, right?" he said. "It was like every half-finished idea in the room suddenly realized it wasn't alone."

He looked at Lila again, softer now.

"And when your voice came in? That's when they felt the permission."

Simon reached down, tapped a slow rhythm against the wooden floor.

"Feels like it's been waiting for a room like this."

No planning. No strategy session. Just breath and presence and the sound of something being made, even now.

Lila pulled a folded scrap of paper from her pocket and began to write. Simon's rhythm deepened. Jonas closed his eyes and let the beat move through his bones.

Not the end of something.

The beginning of return.

Chapter 25 – Voices in the Echo

In the days that followed the gathering, something stayed in motion. Conversations deepened—reflections, messages, long walks, quiet nods. One by one, they circled back to a single idea: it was time to shape something that could last. And now, here they were, gathered to begin what they had all, in their own way, agreed to.

*
**

The room was quiet but not still. Papers lay spread across the re-purposed library table, a mug of tea steaming beside the official state registration form. But no one had touched the pen yet.

They had agreed to meet to shape, align—and to sign.

Scott leaned forward.

"Let's shape the language as carefully as we've shaped the work."

Mira nodded.

"Feels like what we're shaping is more than language—it's direction and alignment. Something that will hold its form as

more voices join."

Lila glanced around the room.

"That question we asked—about making something that helps others remember they had a choice—it made a purpose visible— to create things that help someone else find their own way back to choice."

Jonas added,

"And when those choices include something they've always longed for—something that felt out of reach—it does more than reconnect. It reorients. That's what anchors it as more voices join."

Mira offered,

"And what if that longing—to feel good from the inside—is where reconnection really begins? That feels like humanity to me."

Jonas said quietly,

"Maybe that's what makes someone truly creative—not just what they make, but how they live. When their work or their way of being helps someone else see more than they thought

possible — that's when it starts reshaping the world."

Scott scribbled a few phrases on the corner of a notepad.

"So what do we carry forward? Being creative. Mutual support. Permission. Connection."

There was a pause. A quiet alignment was occurring.
Mira looked toward Anaya.

"Anything missing for you?"

Anaya closed her notebook.

"What you did... it sparked something. The echo holds what's been — some of it beautiful, some of it broken. But it's in the voices that we reshape what's next. If we want more than memory, we have to keep speaking — together."

They let her words settle like light.
Lila whispered,

"That sounds like alliance."

Scott said it aloud, slowly:

"Creative. Humanity. Alliance."

Jonas leaned back slightly.

"So... do we call it that?"

The grin that passed between them said everything.

A small flurry of motion followed—papers gathered, chairs drawn near, pens uncapped. After all the shaping, it was time to begin.

Scott signed first.

Lila followed, then Mira. Jonas last. When he finished, he drew a small symbol beside his name—a spiral, drawn from the inside out.

Jonas reached into his bag and pulled out a small field recorder. He clicked it on and set it in the center of the table.

One by one, they each spoke a sentence—short, true, unrehearsed. A patchwork of intention.

When it was Anaya's turn, she hesitated. Then:

"I'll be here. I'll learn. And when the time's right, I'll teach someone else."

No one spoke after that.

They stepped outside into the deepening dusk. A warm wind carried the scent of jasmine. From somewhere unseen, the faint echo of a drum rose, then faded.

Jonas paused.

The others kept walking, but he stayed behind for a moment.

He closed his eyes.

A voice in the echo.

Waiting.

Ready.

Epilogue

A Different Kind of Inheritance

Humanity has always been the inextricable many.

The songs carried Jonas forward.

The letters, the memories, the long-forgotten dreams—all played their part.

Now, they become something else.

Legacy—not just what's written, recorded, or remembered in isolation.

True legacy is what we share—
held in communion, carried as living memory.

A reconnection that resists the Echo's flattening.

The power of collective remembering.
The restoration of the inextricable many.

Continuing on any stage.
In any studio.
Through any story.

Returning us to the Voice.

It has never lived outside of us—only outside of awareness.
The Echo comes from the world around us—loud, layered, relentless.
But the Voice comes from within.
Not as something separate from others, but as something shared—once remembered.
We have only forgotten how to listen from the inside.

It is recognized.

Recognized in the questions others begin asking. In the conversations that linger long after the gatherings end. In the way Mira rewrites a lesson with her body. In the way Scott turns a system into a sanctuary. In the way Simon and Lila arrive—not needing to be taught, but needing only to magnify the voice already expanding. In the way young Anaya Pierce recognizes the question—and steps into the search for what only the allied many can find again.

And Jonas? He doesn't disappear into the movement. He simply moves out of the center.
He still plays. Still walks the ridge, watches the sky, listens closely.

He brings his fingers to his lips—not to hush, but because something in him remembered that gesture. A kind of acknowledgment that something mattered. A kind of offering.
But the story no longer asks for him to carry it.

It is out there now—magnified by every reconnection.

And what is becoming...

moves like a song that is forever being written.

Composed without authorship, guided by a shared awareness.

Each reconnection adding a verse the world has forgotten—

and a tone once lost now restored.

And if you are quiet enough—still enough—willing to ask a different kind of question—

you might hear it too—not as instruction, but invitation.

you might feel it too—

the warmth of something long forgotten.

in the place you forgot was listening, too.

inside you—

Voices in the Echo.

You're invited.

To listen.

To remember.

To lend your voice.

Visit CreativeHumanityAlliance.org

Back Matter

Acknowledgments

This book could not have been written without the encouragement, insight, and presence of those who reminded me—sometimes with words, sometimes with silence—that the voice inside is worth listening to. Thank you to the creative souls, generous hearts, and kindred spirits who helped shape this journey.

Author's Reflection

While the events and characters in this story are fictional, the emotional truth behind them is real. The Echo is not a villain; it's a force we all reckon with. If you've made it this far, you already know what the Voice is—and why it matters. Thank you for listening so deeply.

About the Author

J. W. Kindbloom is the pen name of a multidisciplinary artist and storyteller who writes from the intersection of memory and imagination, where personal history gives rise to universal stories. Writing under a pen name allows for creative distance and a quieter lens—one that lets the story be larger than the self. Learn more at jwkindbloom.com.

More by J. W. Kindbloom

Coming Spring 2026:

- Voices in the Echo – The next chapter in the journey of Jonas Wilder and those drawn to the edge of silence, where the stories left behind by the Voice begin to echo through new lives, new choices, and an ever-changing world.

Available Now:

- Songs in the Key of Return – An immersive audio companion to The Echo and the Voice, featuring lyrics from the story re-imagined in sound.
- Available here: https://echoandthevoice.com/music

Discussion Questions

1. Which moments in the story felt most familiar or personally resonant?

2. How did the metaphor of "The Echo" show up in your own life experience?

3. What does it mean to you to "listen to the voice inside"?

4. Which character's journey felt most like a reflection— or challenge—of your own?

🎧 Continue the Conversation

Full discussion guides—including bonus questions for book clubs, educators, and creative circles—is available at:

👉 https://jwkindbloom.com/discussion

Whether you're reading alone or together, I'd love to hear what this story sparked in you.

Jonas & Isabel's Reading List

Throughout the story, you may have noticed references—spoken or silent—to the kinds of books that shaped Jonas and Isabel. Some were passed hand-to-hand, others felt like they'd been waiting to be found. Here are a few of the titles that left a mark:

- Jonathan Livingston Seagull by Richard Bach
- One by Richard Bach
- Creative Visualization by Shakti Gawain
- Seven Habits of Highly Effective People by Stephen Covey
- The Souls Code by James Hillman
- The Seven Spiritual Laws of Success by Deepak Chopra
- The 8th Habit by Stephen Covey
- The Awakening of Intelligence by J. Krishnamurti
- Ishmael by Daniel Quinn
- The Story of B by Daniel Quinn
- The Good Life by Scott and Helen Nearing

- The Monkey Wrench Gang by Edward Abbey

- Walden by Henry David Thoreau

- The Prophet by Kahlil Gibran

- Letters to a Young Poet by Rainer Maria Rilke

- The Book of Awakening by Mark Nepo

Some of these books are referenced directly. Others are spirit guides—echoes of the questions Jonas and Isabel were brave enough to ask.

Additional Recommended Reading

Additional Recommended Reading

These titles resonate with the themes of The Echo and the Voice and may offer new paths of reflection:

- Man's Search for Meaning by Viktor E. Frankl
- A Field Guide to Getting Lost by Rebecca Solnit
- The Dispossessed by Ursula K. Le Guin
- The Tao Te Ching by Laozi
- The Little Prince by Antoine de Saint-Exupéry

Praise for The Echo and the Voice

Early responses are coming in from readers who resonate deeply with the story of The Echo and the Voice.

"This book didn't tell me who I was—it reminded me that I already knew."
—Early Reader Reflection

"It felt like someone put words to the quiet truths I've carried for years."
—Advance Praise

"I came looking for a story and left feeling like someone had been listening."
—Reader Reflection

"Like hearing your own heartbeat for the first time—this story doesn't speak over you, it speaks with you."
—Early Reader Reflection

Check back for updates in future editions, or visit JWKindbloom.com for new endorsements as they arrive.

A Final Note

If this book spoke to you, I'd love to hear about it. A brief review or word-of-mouth recommendation helps others find their way here too.

Visit https://echoandthevoice.com to join the mailing list or explore behind-the-scenes content.

Thank you for listening.

— J. W. Kindbloom

Songs from "The Echo and the Voice"

echoandthevoice.com/music

Music, like memory, finds us when we're ready.

The songs that come to life through this story were never meant to stay on the page alone. **"Songs in the Key of Return"** brings them to life as a full-length album—an immersive companion to The Echo and the Voice. If you haven't already found it, you can listen anytime on the music page, or stream it on your preferred platform by searching "Songs in the Key of Return by Jonas Wilder"